# The Bradshaw Mystery

John Waddington-Feather

Feather Books SY3 0BW UK

ISBN:1511908394
ISBN-13:9781511908399

# PROFILE

John Waddington-Feather is an Anglican NSM priest. He has written children's books (one of which was nominated for the Carnegie Medal in 1989) and his verse-play Garlic Lane was awarded the Burton Prize in 1999. He has also written collections of verse and hymns and used to edit the Christian poetry magazine, The Poetry Church. He was a teacher for many years and also ministered in Shrewsbury Prison as a prison visitor and NSM.

Feather Books apologise for any typos which may have been overlooked, however, phrases such as 't'olden days' or 't'church' are intentional and written to reflect the Yorkshire accent of the character concerned.

.

# CHAPTER ONE

It was with mixed feelings that the Revd Detective Inspector Blake Hartley of Keighworth CID and NSM at Ingerworth Parish Church drove across town to the big house near Rombalton Moor. He'd been fast asleep at home when the duty sergeant rang. The housekeeper at The Grange had found her mistress dead.

"Why do they always have to wait till the middle of the night to bump people off, when I'm fast asleep tucked up in bed?" he grumbled to his wife. She was in her dressing-gown, having got up with him to make him a cuppa and get him ready.

"That's the way it's always been, Blake," Mary replied patiently helping him on with his overcoat. "And that's the way it always will be. You chose to be a copper."

"And you chose to marry one, thank goodness," he smiled back, kissing her on the cheek. He slipped his notebook into his pocket and made for the door. "Don't wait up, love. I could be out all night."

"And I've heard that one before," said Mary.

He left her at the door and drove off into the night. Memories came flooding back. He knew the dead woman well. She was Miss

Bradshaw, though he hadn't seen her in years. She'd become a recluse, living with only her housekeeper and gardener, but years before she'd been a leading light in the town like the rest of her family. One of the bright young things of the 1920s and '30s when Keighworth had been one of the richest towns in England; astonishingly wealthy and astonishingly mucky, like all mill-towns.

As she'd grown older Miss Bradshaw had gone odd and locked herself away in the great family house near the moors. Hartley had been there often as a boy. Practically lived there - in the kitchen and servants' quarters. His mother had been the cook before her marriage and had gone there again after her husband had been killed in the army during the war.

Inspector Hartley remembered the house just after the war when much socialising still went on. The Bradshaws were very upper-crustian. Among the richest families in Yorkshire. But those days had long gone. The 1960s had seen off both the rich families and the textile trade. The old families had disappeared one by one along with their wealth and new people, from Asia, had taken their place.

The Grange was the last to survive. All the others had been converted into old people's homes or had disappeared without trace under the demolition hammer. "Executive-style" bungalows had gone up in their stead, crammed like sardines over the old sites and gardens.

But The Grange still stood in its own grounds, and a twenty-acre meadow on the south side still cushioned it from the spreading suburbs of Keighworth. Tall and gabled, its crumbling façade loomed dark and forbidding, like the moors behind. Where the wind swept down from those bleak heights, a protective row of conifers had been planted. They hadn't been touched in years and had grown to an enormous height. They stood shoulder to shoulder and blocked out light on that side of the house.

But the other side, the entrance, was open. Just inside the grounds an overgrown path veered off into a thick clump of rhododendrons. A wormy notice-board still stood there. The wind had ripped off most of the paint, but you could still make out the words: "Tradesmen's Entrance." That was the path Blake Hartley had been forced to use when his mother worked there. Now he drove straight up the drive to the main doors and walked in.

A couple of police cars were parked outside and a constable met him as he left his car. "She's in there, sir," he said, opening the door for the inspector and pointing along the hallway. Hartley thanked him and strode in.

A photographer was taking shots of the body and the forensic team was dusting for fingerprints. Blake's sergeant, Ibrahim Khan, was hiding behind the photographer, keeping as far away from the corpse as possible. It wasn't a pretty sight and Sgt Khan had no stomach for bodies. The mere sight of blood sickened him.

The inspector paused in the doorway and looked slowly round the room, taking in its details. He ran his hand through his thick mane of brown hair, now flecking grey, and sighed. Then his eyes came back to the elderly spinster sprawled lifeless on the floor. Her head had been smashed from behind. Blood still oozed from it and Hartley's gentle eyes narrowed, hardened a moment, then softened again as he murmured a prayer. The priest broke through the policeman's lips.

As he moved into the room, Khan turned to greet him, looking relieved. He came across at once, glad to get away from the body. "Good evening, sir," he began.

"You mean 'Good morning', Khan," Hartley replied, yawning and looking at his watch. "Yesterday went overboard almost an hour ago."

Ibrahim Khan was shorter and darker than his boss. Much younger, too; young enough to have been his son. And there was something of that relationship between them when they were working. Indeed, Hartley was a kind of father-figure to the whole station - except to Superintendent Arthur Donaldson.

Khan was a second generation Asian. His parents had come from Pakistan to Bradford in the early 1950s. They'd done well. So had Khan, who'd won a place at the local grammar school then gone on to Oxford. After graduation he trained at the Police College, then served on the beat in downtown London for two years with the Met before going back north. He hadn't long been married and lived on the opposite side of town to Hartley, not far from The Grange.

"Found owt?" asked the inspector.

"Only this," said Khan, holding up a plastic bag with a slip of paper inside. "It was under the chair where the old lady had been sitting. It's a betting slip, sir."

"Surprised you know what one of them is," said Hartley. "You a good Muslim and non-gambler."

Khan smiled. "I'm surprised you yourself recognised it, sir. You a good Christian priest and all that."

The inspector grunted and knelt by the body, glancing at it briefly. It was Miss Bradshaw all right. She looked as arrogant as ever. But death had cut her down to size. Her dentures had slipped out, giving her a comical look. Khan kept his distance.

The old lady's handbag had burst open on the floor. It smelled strongly of scent. Hartley could see a bottle of it, and other oddments, in the bag. A set of keys was there also, and a fob-watch.

"We'll have a look-see inside that bag when the photographer's done," said Hartley, standing up. "Any sign of a break-in, Khan? Anything disturbed?"

"No, sir. Everything seems OK. We'll know better when it gets light and we can see outside."

"Who found her?"

"The housekeeper, Mrs Goodwin, sir," said Khan. He lowered his voice and looked in the direction of the kitchen. "She's in there, sir. Very calm, considering what's happened." Then he added, "I think she's a bit simple, sir."

"But not as daft as she looks," commented the inspector. "I've known her for years."

"And she's been drinking, sir," added Khan. "Her breath nearly knocked me over!" Then his eyes wandered magnetically back to the body and he blenched.

"You seem as if you could do with a drink yourself, Khan," observed his boss. "I should go outside and get some fresh air. You look as if you're going to throw up."

Mrs Goodwin was pouring herself another gin as Hartley entered the kitchen. The nearly empty bottle was on the table. Another one stuck out of the waste-bin.

He knew Lizzie Goodwin well, but hadn't seen her for years. They'd got on in a rum sort of way when he'd been a lad. She'd pulled his leg unmercifully then. The way adolescent boys came in for ribbing by the servants. She'd been a scullery maid then, but as the other servants left, she'd stayed on, rising through the ranks to housekeeper by the time she was forty. Only she and a half-witted gardener called Woodley remained of the old staff, which had once numbered twenty.

She was about ten years older than the inspector, into her sixties. She was a big woman, mannish and powerful with close-cropped steel-grey hair. Her movements were slow and deliberate like a man's, too.

Yet when the inspector had first known her she'd had the bloom of youth on her. She'd been handsome. Full-blooded. Attractive. There was still a suggestion of it in her ruddy features and dark eyes. But age had taken its toll. Her skin had coarsened. Time and smoking had etched lines across her face.

She'd lived at The Grange all her working life, coming as a girl into service from a farm over the eastern side of Yorkshire. She'd married the chauffeur, but he'd died early on in their marriage. They'd no children. When Blake had first known her she was living in the garret with another maid. Now she had one of the two lodge cottages at the old gates. The gardener, Sammy Woodley, lived opposite, in the other. He and an old biddy in the housing estate down the road were her only friends.

She looked up as Blake came through the door and pushed her glass to one side trying to hide it. She wasn't drunk and, as Khan had remarked, looked surprisingly calm, though she scowled as he entered.

"Hello, Lizzie," he said affably. "It must be years since we last met."

She grunted.

"Sad do this, isn't it?" he began, taking out his notebook.

She looked at him keenly, then went over to the stove and began to mash some tea. "Tha'rt Nellie Hartley's lad, aren't tha? I didn't recognise thee at first, but I heard tha were coming. Tha'll have some tea?"

"Thank you," he said and opened his book. "Lizzie, I've got to ask you some questions." He paused to sip his tea then said, "There seems to be some discrepancy…"

"Stop talking fancy. I don't know what tha means," she broke in. "Talk like tha used to when thy mother worked here."

The inspector coughed and smiled. "There's summat doesn't tie up," he said. "It was some time - after eleven - before you phoned us to tell us about Miss Bradshaw. Yet you told the officer you'd got back here from bingo around ten o'clock. Why?"

She didn't answer at once. She looked agitated and fiddled with her hankie and blew her nose. Then she looked up suddenly and said angrily, "Because I didn't find her straight away. That's why. I thought she were in bed. She grumbled like hell if I woke her up when I came in, so I came in here to make sure she were fast asleep." Lizzie drank her tea noisily before she added, "In any case, I had a bit of a fright coming back tonight, an' I had to have a drink to pull meself together."

"Fright?"

"Somebody dashed out of t'gates just as I were coming in. Nearly knocked me over. I thought it were Sammy Woodley at first, 'cos he carried a spade, but it weren't." She broke off and began munching a biscuit loudly. It grated on Hartley and he sensed she knew it for she made it last. "I bet it were one o' them chaps from t'estate pinching our plants. They're allus thieving from t'gardens."

She took another biscuit and began chomping again, watching Blake closely all the time. He said nothing but continued writing in his book. His silence forced her to speak again. She was uncomfortable with his silences.

"It were when I started me rounds I found her. I'd a right shock I can tell thee. Opening t'drawing-room door an' seeing her there wi' her head all bashed in an' covered in blood!"

"Yet you didn't contact us then."

"I phoned Mr Fawcett - her nephew. Tha remembers him? He told me to ring him straight away if owt happened to her. Like she were taken ill. But neither of us expected owt like this."

"What did he say?" asked Hartley.

"It were a woman who answered t'phone."

"His wife?"

"No. He's never married."

Lizzie Goodwin glanced across quickly, but the inspector remained deadpan.

"She said Mr Fawcett wasn't there but would be back shortly. She told me to ring t'police, which I did. She said he'd drive over when he got in. I've been expecting him any time."

Inspector Hartley drained his cup and stood up. He put his notebook away and she looked relieved. She followed him to the door and they almost collided when he stopped to ask, "Oh, just one more question, Lizzie. Whenever you phoned Mr Fawcett to tell him his aunt was ill, did you let her know?"

The housekeeper flushed. "After she'd gone odd, there were things I kept from her. She'd such a vile temper. Tha couldn't reason wi' her. I turned to Mr Fawcett for help when she were like that. He's allus been good to me. More than her. More than them all. So it were him I took notice of. Not her. If tha sees what I mean."

Inspector Hartley smiled. "I think I do, Lizzie," he said quietly. "You and he always did get on well, didn't you?"

Then he turned and left her to her biscuits and the bottle on the shelf.

# CHAPTER TWO

Sammy Woodley, Miss Bradshaw's gardener, couldn't be contacted the night of the murder. And her nephew, Peter Fawcett, was also unavailable. The inspector particularly wanted to see both of them. Fawcett phoned to say his car had broken down the other side of Skiproyd. Could he come to the station the next day when it had been repaired? Inspector Hartley told him to stay at home. He'd visit him there. To tell the truth, Hartley was curious to see where he lived. He knew Grasby Manor from his youth, but only from a distance. He'd never been inside.

Blake knew that Fawcett would be able to tell him a great deal about his aunt which Lizzie had kept quiet about. In particular, the inspector wanted to find out more about the old lady's personal life. As they drove to the Manor the next day, he and Khan chatted about the case. The day before, he'd left his sergeant with Lizzie to see if he could get anything more out of her. He'd drawn a blank. "Didn't get a peep," he said, looking out of the window. "She answered in words of one syllable, then became downright rude - racist. She doesn't care much for folk of my colour."

"I hope you're big enough not to let it worry you. You've had it all before, Khan," said Hartley gently. "To the likes of Lizzie even going to Bradford is like a trip abroad. Places like London are on another planet." His sergeant smiled, and Hartley quipped, "She might be right there." But Khan wasn't impressed, so Hartley said more seriously, "You're not the only one who's had to face prejudice, Khan. I had to as a young copper. Admittedly it was prejudice of a different sort, but it bit just as deep. I could have ended up all bitter and twisted if I'd let it get on top of me."

They drove in silence as his words sank in.

"When I was a lad," he continued, "it mattered who your parents were and where you were brought up. Which school you went to - even how you spoke. If you didn't fit you'd had it. The British class system ruled the roost then, and still does in some parts. But now it's often something else. The colour of your skin, how much you earn, how big your house and car are. It's almost a sin to be poor now, especially if you're on benefits. Aye, lad, you'll always have prejudice. It's everywhere and I bet you have it in your own community."

Ibrahim Khan nodded and they both fell silent again, watching the long grey-stone terraced houses slide by. The road north from Keighworth was lined with trees. It was a long straight road, focusing northwards on the hills and farmland leading to the Dales.

The river sliced the valley in two, separating green meadows from the rough pasturage rising sharply to the moors. Black gritty drystone walls varicosed the hillsides for some miles out of Keighworth till they reached Skiproyd. There they turned astonishingly white in limestone country; sharpening the very light. Along the valley, the crests were tinged red with dead bracken. Higher still, mournful clouds slouched over the Pennines from Lancashire, threatening as always more rain..

As they drove, Blake Hartley pointed out landmarks from his past. His mother's grandparents had come from the Dales, leaving their tiny small-holdings to find work and a steady wage in the mills at Keighworth. Money came more easily there, if less healthily.

He glanced across at his sergeant still silent.

"You've got one thing in your favour, Khan," he said.

"What's that, sir?"

"Education. I'd have liked to have gone to university, but never got the chance. We couldn't afford it after my dad was killed. I had to leave school in the sixth-form. Went straight into the army to do my National Service. I learned a lot about life there. Joined the Force when I came out and never looked back. Never regretted it."

Then he returned to murder case they were on.

"This chap Fawcett we're going to interview. Like I said, I've known him since I was a lad. He's had more chances in life than you and me put together. No prejudice to face. Born with a silver spoon in his mouth. Left a fortune by his grandad - but he still turned out a wrong 'un. Greedy as they come. Always wanted more. And when he couldn't get it the right way, he took it t'other. Aye, I've know him all my life. Long enough to feel that somehow he's connected with his aunt's murder."

Sergeant Khan looked across surprised. "Why do you think that, sir?"

The inspector shrugged his shoulders, and wouldn't meet the other's eye.

"Oh, I don't know, Khan. Just a gut-feeling."

"You've something personal against him, sir. Haven't you?" said Khan watching his boss keenly

Hartley shifted uneasily. "You might say that."

Khan waited. It would all come out.

"When I was a lad," said Hartley, a mile or two further on, "my mother was in service at The Grange. I had to go there each day straight from school till she'd finished work. She was the cook for the Bradshaws, so I always had to stay in the kitchen or servants' quarters. That's how I came to know Lizzie Goodwin. But when the Bradshaws were away, I wandered round their part of the house. And I envied them. Oh, how I envied them! All their wealth and finery; all their self-confidence."

He said nothing for a while, apparently concentrating on the road which had become more crowded with traffic heading for the market at Skiproyd. Then he continued, "I was always kept in line at The Grange. Made to feel my place like my mother. Especially by

Fawcett. He's a bit older than me and he loved lording it about the place. He never let me forget I was working-class. That I was the underdog."

"I know the feeling, sir," said Khan quietly. He was learning much about his boss, about life in general.

"For much of the time, Fawcett was away at boarding school and university, but when he came for the holidays he had the run of the place. He was the only grandchild and they doted on him. For me, the worst part was he never had to work hard for success. Paid for at a good public school which had fixed places at Cambridge. He was clever - too clever by half as it turned out. Good at sport - he'd a blue for rowing - an athlete, took a first in languages. You name it, he was the cat's whiskers. He didn't have to try, even with women, like you and me." Hartley turned and smiled. "They flung themselves at his feet."

"How comes it he went wrong, sir?"

"Spoiled rotten. Grew up enjoying the good life and knew no other. He always wanted more. He'd the greedy mill-master streak in him. Rumour had it he put a girl in the family way. One of the servants, though we never knew which one. It was all hushed up and there was never a baby in the house. Then he went into the army like the rest of us. Struck it lucky there. He was attached to the embassy in Karachi. Signed on for a short service commission and stayed there till he came back to Keighworth."

"To the family business?"

"Aye. But not for long. He knew which way the wind was blowing. Mills were going bust all over the place. He sold out and began dabbling in shady property deals among other things. He lived abroad in Spain for some years till his partner got bumped off. Interpol never did get to the bottom of that. After that he returned to England, bought Grasby Manor, and played the country gentleman. I've heard he's into antiques now in Leeds. Now can you understand why I somehow think he's linked to his aunt's murder, Khan?"

Khan didn't understand, but he'd heard enough to know there was more to this case than met the eye. Something deep between his boss and Fawcett. He asked if the old lady had any other near relatives.

"None," said the inspector. "Fawcett's the only one. He'll come in for everything. The lines of Lady Luck always fall right for his sort."

"The Will of Allah," murmured Khan.

"More likely the will of his aunt. He'll collar the lot!" replied Hartley.

By now they were approaching the outskirts of Skiproyd. Its ancient church stood at the end of a wide main street, cobbled and tree-lined. Behind the church loomed Skiproyd Castle, grey and heavy.

It was market-day and traders' vans were parked the length of the street. By them was a collection of open stalls. Everything was sold there: pots, fent-ends, gum-boots, outdoor clothing - and cheap antiques. A van blocked their way and while they waited for it to back they casually scanned the crowds.

Suddenly Hartley nudged his sergeant and pointed. By one stall was Woodley, the missing gardener. As Hartley leaned across for a better look, the gardener saw him. He was carrying a vase and haggling with the stall-holder who dealt in cheap antiques, many of them imitation. When he recognised the inspector, Woodley got rid of his vase, pushing it under the stall. Then he bolted into the crowd.

The detectives leapt out and gave chase, but it was no use. The crowd was too dense. Frustrated they went back to the stall, where the inspector showed his ID. It had a marked effect on the stall-holder. His face set and he said insolently, "What yer want? It's all clean here."

He was small and shabby, getting on in years, but as alert as a weasel. He kept glancing beyond Hartley across the road. Probably to see if Woodley had got safely away. He had a leathery grimy face under his cap. The sort of face produced by cheap soap and a bad diet.

"Who was the chap you were speaking with just now?" asked Hartley.

"What chap?"

"The one trying to sell you a vase," The other smirked then looked blank. The inspector lost his rag and drew closer to the old man. "Come off it! You know who I mean. Don't waste my time or I'll book you for obstruction!"

The other changed tack. "Oh, him?" he said as if suddenly enlightened. "Dunno, boss. Just some'dy who turned up. Folk do that, y'know, when they're hard up. They'll sell you owt."

"Specially if they've nicked it," said Khan.

The stall-holder flashed him an angry look. "Nicked it! Give me a break, boss. I never handle stuff I know what's hot. It's more than me licence is worth."

"But if someone just happens along and shoves a bargain under your nose, you don't refuse," said Hartley. "No questions, no sweat."

He moved round the stall and yanked out the vase they'd seen. It was a beauty. The real thing and worth a bomb. He held it up. A crowd of curious onlookers had begun to gather. "Looks a bit more classy than the rest of your stuff," said the inspector. "You wouldn't find this in Woolworths."

The dealer licked his lips and lowered his voice. "Well…er…like I said, when folks is hard up they'll trade you owt. Family heirlooms, the lot, just as long as they can get their hands on a bit o' ready cash. I help 'em out till they can buy it back."

"Got any names?" asked Khan.

The dealer fished out a greasy notebook and handed it over. Hartley thumbed through it.

"You've got somebody here called Woodley. You've done quite a bit of trade with him over the years. And surprise, surprise the chap you were talking with when we arrived is called Sammy Woodley," said Hartley. "Now isn't that just a coincidence? Right. Let's start again."

The dealer began to look scared. He was still glancing across the road and Hartley wondered why.

"OK, boss. OK," he said. "I got into a panic when you coppers popped up. Aye, he's called Woodley, but I don't know much about him, 'cept he's got a bird in Skiproyd and comes here reg'lar. We don't ask questions in this business. What you don't know, you can't tell, eh? He's been flogging me bits and pieces for years. Says he's trading them for an old woman in Keighworth. As far as I know his slate's clean, so I don't ask no more." He took his notebook from the inspector and opened it for him to see. "It's all there, boss. 'Sam Woodley, Grange Cottage, Moor End Road, Ruddledene, Keighworth.' Straight up like I said."

Inspector Hartley looked at him more closely. "Your name's Cudworth, isn't it? Now I remember. Eli Cudworth from Colne.

The old man looked surprised. "That's right, boss. How did yer know?"

Blake tapped his forehead. "Memory, Eli. Mr Plod's memory goes back a long way. You were in the Whitworth gang who went round nicking lead from church roofs."

The dealer looked more agitated than ever. "What's past is past, boss. I did my bird for that twenty years ago. I've gone straight ever since. This stuff's clean an' you know it. Either charge me or clear off. Yer getting me a bad name. Yer putting customers off, standing there rolling out the past like soggy wallpaper. Give me a break!"

Inspector Hartley nodded. He began to feel sorry for him, a worn out old lag reduced to trading in cheap antiques.

"OK, Eli, I'll believe you. Thousands wouldn't," said Hartley. "But we haven't come all the way to Skiproyd to nick you for trading stolen goods. It's more serious. Murder. The old lady killed in Keighworth yesterday. Woodley was her gardener."

Cudworth grimaced. "I read all about it. It were all over t'front page. And she were Woodley's boss! Now look, boss, I don't want any dealings wi' murder. Perhaps I don't ask the questions I oughter, but I don't have no truck wi' murder."

"Then tell us where Woodley hangs out," said Khan.

The dealer looked over his shoulder anxiously, then whispered, "Try the Black Bull around mid-day, boss. He sups in the tap there. But for God's sake don't ever say I told yer. He's crazy and he's got some crazy friends. I don't want them leaning on me."

They left the old man and returned to their car. As they walked back, Inspector Hartley glanced across the road in the direction Cudworth had been looking. Scowling over a screen of house-sale notices was a pair of Asians. The detective looked at the office sign above: "Quereshi Brothers, Estate Agents and Developers." When his gaze dropped to the window again, the two men had disappeared.

"I'd like to bet our man's in there," said Khan nodding at the offices. "The Quereshis are as bent as corkscrews. Shall we go in and have a look, sir?"

Hartley shook his head. "They've seen us. Best let the dust settle and call at the Black Bull on our way back. We can nab Woodley then."

He put the car into gear and they drove off, nudging their way through the traffic till they were clear of the town. When they'd gone, the two Asians left their offices and crossed the road. They spoke briefly to Eli Cudworth then dragged him across the road before bundling him inside. They pushed him, pleading, into a chair. Then Woodley slunk into the room, brandishing an iron bar.

# CHAPTER THREE

Leaving Skiproyd, the detectives drove through superb Dales countryside. It was the first sunny day of spring and the air had the bite of a ripe apple. Now they were into limestone country, driving through corridors of white winding walls, alongside fields emerald with new grass. Here and there the land was broken by the black turn of a plough.

The sun beat down hotly and Hartley wound down the window. For some miles they followed the Aire. Nearer, parallel with the road, the Leeds-Liverpool Canal bolted straight for the horizon before it cut through the hills into Lancashire. Freshly-painted barges and pleasure-craft chugged up and down on their first outings of the season. It was idyllic. Hard to imagine they were on a murder hunt.

Inspector Hartley turned off abruptly at Garthrop, going the long way round to Grasby. He'd ceased humming to himself for some time, concentrating more and more on his driving mirror. Khan asked why they'd turned off, sensing something was wrong.

Blake nodded at his mirror. "We're being followed," he said. "A black Merc's been behind us ever since we left Skiproyd. The driver keeps using his car phone. My guess is he's relaying where we are to someone ahead, and there's no prize for saying who."

Hartley slowed down. So did the car behind. When they left the main road, the Mercedes followed them into the winding lane to Grasby.

After a couple of miles, Hartley put his foot down. The walls were high, so that at times the car behind was out of sight. But the Mercedes hung on and he couldn't shake it off till they reached the farm next to the Manor.

The inspector took a deep breath and slewed into a farmyard, hiding behind the barn. He switched off his engine and waited. "I only hope old Fothergill isn't about," he said. "We never did get on!"

They could hear the Mercedes skidding round the bends as it tried to hang on. It approached the farm and sped past. They waited some moments then Hartley switched on his engine. "Two can play their game," he said, smiling quietly to himself "They can't turn till they reach the Manor. We'll let them announce they've lost us, then put in an appearance."

Just as they were leaving the farmyard, a grizzled old head popped over a stable door. It was Josiah Fothergill. "Who the bloody hell does tha think tha art? Stirling Moss? This is private property. Not a bloody pit-stop. Driving like bloody maniacs!"

The inspector accelerated, ducking as they went past the old man. Fothergill shook his fist. "I've got thy bloody number!" he yelled after them. "I'll report thee to t'police!"

They didn't see the Mercedes again till they reached the Manor. It stood in the drive alongside a vintage 1939 Alvis Drophead Coupé, an exclusive red 4.3 litre model. It gleamed as a chauffeur sponged it down, washing its mud-splashed headlights carefully. It had been driven recently - and fast.

The Manor was an elegant stone-mullioned building, three storeys high; a rambling place with virginia creeper over its frontage. Its oldest parts were Elizabethan, but it had been added to over the centuries. An earlier building, a fortified house, had stood on the site; but that had long gone. A bit of its moat still remained as a duck-pond near the east wing.

Fawcett kept it immaculate. In all things he was fastidious. The sanded drive was swept daily. The lawn was manicured. Mottling it was a show of late daffodils trumpeting the sun. Around the perimeter of the house and garages ran a high wall, which sheltered a kitchen garden at the rear. It also served to keep out unwanted visitors.

Before the front entrance a pillared porch covered a solid oak door, studded and barred with wrought iron. At the base of the pillars crouched a couple of stone lions. Near them sat a very flesh-and-blood Irish wolfhound. It got to its feet immediately they left their car and began growling.

"Here, Jack! Heel!" ordered the man cleaning the car. The brute stopped growling and slunk towards him. It crouched at his feet watching every move the detectives made.

The servant did likewise.

He was well-built, swarthy and hard-faced. Weather-beaten. More used to outdoor work than driving cars. He could have been a gamekeeper - or poacher. He'd a red neckerchief tied round his neck and wore a collarless shirt and no jacket. He stopped cleaning but stayed by the car watching them as they approached, saying nothing, only scowling. And there was more than a hint of cruelty behind the malice of his scowl.

When they were close enough he growled, "What yer want?"

The inspector showed his ID, watching the dog at his feet all the time. Given half a chance, he felt the servant would have set it on them. The other glanced at his ID and his lip curled insolently. He remained mute, standing with his hands on his hips waiting for them to speak.

"Inspector Hartley and Sergeant Khan, Keighworth CID. Mr Fawcett's expecting us," said Hartley.

The chauffeur jerked his head towards the door. "Yer'll find t'gaffer inside," he said. "Make sure yer ring t'bell first and wait. There's another couple inside like this one. They'll have yer as soon as look at yer if yer try to walk straight in. They don't take to strangers."

"So it seems," said Hartley, and when they were out of earshot he murmured, "And the dogs aren't the only ones either."

As they moved off, the wolfhound stood up and growled again. The servant shouted at it and it fell silent. He watched them all the way to the door till they rang the bell. At the first chime all hell was let loose. More hounds inside hurled themselves at the door inside and began barking and snarling. A woman's voice called them off and the racket ceased.

After the reception outside the detectives expected a female equivalent of the handyman greeting them, but when the door opened they were in for a surprise. They were greeted by an Asian woman, raven-haired and beautiful. She'd everything a woman needed, with rather more where a woman needs it most. She wore a sari perfectly. It matched her warm skin, which in turn emphasised her dazzling teeth. And they heightened the redness of her full lips.

The smile she gave was well practised, alluring. Her deep brown eyes, too, were used to handling men. She could melt them with a single look and regarded the detectives with a measured stare, reading them as they read her. But there was a difference. They tried to turn too many pages!

All below her smile was even more magnetic and before he could check himself, Inspector Hartley had dropped his eyes to her low-cut top. It held an abundance no man could resist.

Then the inspector realised where his eyes had wandered and lifted them quickly. She continued smiling, knowing full well the effect she was having. Young Khan continued to gaze his fill while she spoke to his boss. She transferred her gaze suddenly and caught him unawares.

"You must be Inspector Hartley," she said. "And you?"

She faltered.

"Er... Detective Sergeant Khan," he replied embarrassed, bringing his eyes up to meet hers.

She spoke flawless English like Khan. But there was a difference. Hers was upper-class. Fawcett's brand of English. Khan's was like Hartley's. Flat-vowelled, hinting at back-street Bradford. She opened the door wider and let them in. They were clearly expected.

They followed her to the lounge through an oak-panelled hallway. She was as beautiful in retreat as she was in advancing, and she knew it as she swayed gracefully with every step. Like many beautiful women she was more provocative dressed than undressed, hinting at hidden delights. Behind the trio slouched the hounds, shadowing their ankles. When they entered the lounge, the brutes took up their post by the door, blocking any retreat.

Fawcett was awaiting them. He stood, master of the house, lounging nonchalantly by a huge open fireplace. The mantelpiece was stiff with priceless antiques; a magnificent rococo French clock the centrepiece. Above it on the wall hung the portrait of a man in eighteenth century dress. One of the original owners. It gave tone to the room and was the ancestor of someone clearly not a Fawcett, for the eyes were too gentle and the face too genteel.

The lounge was decorated in period wallpaper and delicate Italian plasterwork. Hepplewhite chairs were set in just the right places, and to one side stood a Sheraton side-table laden with drinks. Fawcett had taste all right and indulged it to the full.

The woman completed the decoration. She took up her place by his side as they went in. They contrasted greatly in some respects. In others they were alike. They both liked the good things of life and had been used to them from birth.

She was dark-skinned, full mouthed and nubile. He was much older and fair-skinned, though tanned. His hair was grey at the temples making him look distinguished. He had a commanding presence, but his pale blue eyes were restless. Calculating. They smiled suavely one moment, then the next they blazed evil. And his lips, though thin, were sensual, lascivious.

Peter Fawcett was older than Blake Hartley, but he'd kept his figure better. He groomed himself to excess and was a health fanatic; jogging just so many miles each day and fastidious with his diet. He had his own gym in the house and went regularly to one in Leeds where he worked. Yet the wrinkling about his neck betrayed his age and he did his best to hide it with high collars and cravats.

He was at ease anywhere and could captivate strangers at first meeting with his easy manner and boyish chuckle. But once you'd rumbled him, he was repulsive. Blake Hartley had rumbled him long ago.

"Well, well, well," he said smoothly, "Blake Hartley… after all these years. And *Inspector* Blake Hartley to boot. They tell me you're ordained, too. You have done well for yourself, if I may say so. Congratulations. A policeman-priest! Only the Church of England could have laid that on."

He paused to size up the inspector. There was mockery in his eyes.

"I've heard much about you one way or another over the years, especially recently, which makes it rather sad meeting again under these circumstances. Poor auntie. I still can't register she's dead."

He made no attempt to shake the inspector's hand, and despite his welcome his attitude was patronising. His voice had sarcastic overtones.

"I'm very sorry about Miss Bradshaw, sir," began Blake. "Her death came as something of a shock to me, too, knowing her so well in the past."

Fawcett sighed, pursed his lips and adjusted his cravat. "It would never have happened if she'd taken my advice and moved into a home. I'd been trying to persuade her to move for years. The Grange was far too big for her. But you know how stubborn old people can be." He turned to the woman. "But I'm not being a very good host, am I? Jay, be a darling and fix the inspector and sergeant a drink. A beer perhaps?"

The woman moved towards the Sheraton, but Hartley stopped her. "No, thank you. We're not drinking."

Fawcett smiled. "Of course. Quite right. You're on duty."

"Not only that, sir. It's Lent. I give up drink in Lent."

Fawcett raised his eyebrows. "Ah, yes. I was forgetting. I'm afraid I'm very much a pagan, Hartley. I was never much good at that sort of thing. They tried hard with me at school. I even won a divinity prize of some sort. But your sergeant?"

"It's Ramadan," said Khan.

"A Muslim. I should have known better. I'm sorry," said Fawcett and laughed lightly. "You'll gather I'm not very religious," then added quickly,"though I respect religious belief, of course."

"Of course," said Khan, and matched Fawcett's smile.

Just for an instant Fawcett was lost for a reply. He hadn't expected

Khan's riposte. He ignored it and said, "But you won't object if I have a snifta, will you? It's about medicine time."

He nodded at the woman who poured him a stiff whisky before fixing herself a gin and tonic. She brought him his whisky and stayed at his side, watching the detectives closely as she sipped her drink.

"A wee drop o'stag's breath soon puts the world to rights," he said swirling his malt whisky round his mouth before swallowing. "Now, Hartley, what can I do for you? The quicker we get through this miserable business, the better, eh? I don't suppose you enjoy doing it any more than myself. I'm afraid I won't be of much help, though."

"Oh, I don't know, sir. You'll be surprised. Every bit of information helps. Like a jig-saw," said Hartley, taking out his notebook.

"I suppose so," said Fawcett, then added. "By the way, Hartley, your superintendent speaks highly of you." Inspector Hartley looked up. Fawcett lied. He was trying to pull rank. Hartley and his Super while not exactly at daggers drawn certainly had their hands on the scabbard. They held each other in mutual contempt.

Fawcett was one of the Masonic clique Donaldson mixed with. He was always dropping his name, and played golf regularly with Fawcett at some posh club the other side of Leeds, well away from Keighworth. Donaldson was always trying to impress Hartley with the names he met there. But Blake Hartley didn't play golf and he'd never been impressed by the likes of Fawcett, and he never dropped names.

When he turned to his notebook again he went straight to the point. "Whose is the Mercedes outside, sir?" he asked.

Fawcett frowned and glanced out of the window. "I can't see what that has to do with my aunt's murder," he said sharply, "but if you must know, it's mine. Or rather it belongs to the business I run in Leeds. Two of my assistants have it for our weekly get-together. Why do you ask?"

"I was curious, that's all, sir,"

Fawcett nodded. But clearly didn't like the next question and he didn't like the deliberate way Hartley was writing down everything he said. "When were you last at Miss Bradshaw's, sir?"

"The day she died," he replied, frowning. "Popped over to see her as I always did, on my way to work. She seemed in high spirits, which was unusual."

"Oh? Why?"

"She'd become very crotchety. Old age, I suppose. I take it that it'll be in order for me to go down there later today and sort a few things out?"

"Of course, sir," said Hartley. "Let me know if anything is missing, please."

"I'm afraid I can't help you there, Hartley," said Fawcett airily. "Ask the housekeeper or Woodley. They'll tell you. They knew more about her personal effects than me." Then he turned to Sergeant Khan.

"May I ask if you have any idea who did it, sergeant?"

"None," said Khan. "There doesn't appear to be any motive."

"My dear sergeant, there's a motive for every crime; otherwise it wouldn't be committed," quipped Fawcett, and gave his soft chuckle.

Hartley broke in with, "Forgive me asking, sir, but I assume you'll inherit everything."

The smile left Fawcett's face. He took a sip of whisky and said brusquely, "That's somewhat personal, isn't it? I can't see what it has to do with your investigation. But yes. I'll inherit everything, I suppose. I'm her only relative. But what on earth has that to do with her death?" He burst out laughing. "Unless you think I did it! I hope you're not being serious. The idea's preposterous!"

Hartley remained impassive. "I'm serious all right, sir. You've just said there has to be a motive for every crime. Greed accounts for many crimes and I'm trying to establish the motive for your aunt's murder."

Fawcett was wrong-footed. He threw the inspector a quick glance and looked at his watch. "I'd rather like another drink, Jay," he said. Then turned again to Hartley. "Is there anything else, inspector? I'm having lunch with my assistants, and if I'm to visit The Grange I really must fly."

"I think that will be all for the time being, sir," said Hartley, putting away his notebook. "Unless Sergeant Khan has any questions."

Khan shook his head. While his boss had been questioning Fawcett, he'd been admiring the furniture. It didn't escape Fawcett's notice.

"I see you're admiring my bits and pieces, sergeant," said Fawcett. "Know anything about antiques?"

"Only in a general way, sir," Khan replied. "It's my wife who's the expert. But I do like your Chippendale chairs."

"Hepplewhite, actually," corrected Fawcett. "Yes. They are rather beautiful, aren't they? If you're ever in Leeds do call in at my place and feel free to browse around. I've a wide selection." He gave the sergeant a card as he ushered them to the door.. "Jay here manages the shop. She'll be delighted to show you and your wife around."

The hounds got to their feet and followed them out. They were stopped at the door where the hound outside took over. There was no sign of the Mercedes, but the handyman was still polishing the Alvis. He said nothing as they approached, keeping his head well down; but once they'd passed they felt his stare all the way back to their car.

As they pulled clear, they glimpsed Fawcett standing at the French window sipping his whisky, his arm round the Asian woman at his side. He waved and seemed to be laughing at something she said. But Hartley ignored him and drove on.

"See what I mean when I spoke about him earlier?" he murmured. Khan nodded.

They spoke little all the way to Skiproyd where they called in at The Bull for lunch. There was no sign of Woodley. They had a bite then hung around for some time, hoping he'd turn up, but he didn't. They decided that somehow he'd been tipped off and they left an hour later. When they returned to their car round the back, its door had been forced. In the rear seat lay Eli Cudworth, badly beaten up and unconscious.

# CHAPTER FOUR

Ibrahim and Semina Khan lived in a large Edwardian house. It had gone to seed like its previous owners, an elderly couple. But the Khans had begun restoring it and furnishing it with period furniture. Their house was in Ruddledene; not far from The Grange. In fact, just beyond the ageing council estate built in the 1930s adjacent to The Grange. The Bradshaws had made a killing on the land they sold. But they lived to regret it. Leastways, Miss Bradshaw did.

The day after his visit to Grasby Manor, Sergeant Khan and his wife attended a family get-together in Bradford at an expensive tandoori restaurant. One of the best in England's curry capital.

The private dining room was divided into largish alcoves, which could be reserved at a price. Each party could eat privately, screened from the others by ornate trellising and climbing plants. At intervals along the walls hung large gilt-framed mirrors to give the impression of space. Indian sitars played subdued background music to the guests as they ate.

It was still Ramadan and as they hadn't eaten since morning, the Khan family did full justice to their meal. However, they'd been disturbed by a noisy party next door, who talked too loudly and laughed too heartily. They were awaiting the arrival of someone and spoke the dialect of northern Pakistan, up near the Afghan border. All were expensively dressed and flashed expensive gold watches on their wrists and rings on their fingers

Ibrahim had turned his back to the group like the rest of his family. Yet he could see what was going on through the mirror opposite. His eyes were drawn there after a loud outburst of greetings as someone entered. To his surprise, he saw the beautiful Asian woman he'd met at Grasby.

She was accompanied by a tall well-built man, handsome but with a hard face. The sort of face Ibrahim had put behind bars. The rest of the group stood when the couple entered. They clearly had clout, and were treated with great respect by the louts who'd been mouthing off all night.

"What are you looking at?" asked Semina, curious why her husband was staring so hard.

"That woman I told you about. The one we met at Grasby Manor yesterday. She's just walked in! Joined the crowd next door."

They were interrupted by a waitress serving them coffee. Khan asked her who the couple was who'd just come in. The waitress glanced across and lowered her voice, as if afraid to be overheard.

"She's Jay Hussein," she whispered. "And the man she's with is Abdul Quereshi. Bad news both of them. We don't like having them here. But what can we do? If we complained, they'd turn nasty. If you see what I mean."

Khan nodded. "The Quereshis were involved in some sort of protection racket a few years ago, weren't they?"

The waitress didn't say anything. She merely nodded in reply and moved off quickly, afraid to say more while Quereshi and his gang were still there.

Two of them were immediately behind the trellis where Khan sat. He could hear every word they said though they were screened from each other. They were seated away from Jay Hussein, at the far end of the alcove while she and her escort chatted with another group. The two next to Khan were talking about her father. One had recently returned from Karachi and was up-dating the other. He hadn't met Jay Hussein before though he'd heard much about her. Khan pricked up his ears.

"So that's her," said the character nearest Khan. "She's every bit as beautiful as I'd heard. Pity about her father, though."

"What about him?" asked the other.

"He ran into trouble the last time he did the Quetta run. Made the mistake of going there alone and trusting his suppliers. Trust a Pathan! He must have been crazy! He never came back. Should have stuck to our side of the border."

"They say he's got millions stashed away in Karachi and the beautiful Miss Hussein will come in for everything. Whoever wins her fair hand scoops the jackpot."

"Where does she live? In Bradford?"

"No. Somewhere out in the country up the Dales, with an old friend of her father's. Lived with him years. Ever since she came to school in Britain."

"Know him?"

"Wish I did. He was the broker for her dad. He's got fingers in every pie from Bradford to Karachi. The Big White Chief they call him. Right at the top. He works with the Quereshis, but he's the one who calls the shots."

The conversation dried up suddenly, as Quereshi himself waved them over to join him. Shortly after, the whole party left and the Khans were left in peace.

Sgt Khan couldn't get to the office fast enough the next day to tell Hartley what he'd learned. But as he entered he was pulled up short. His boss was engrossed in the pathology report on Miss Bradshaw. Worse, he was holding up a couple of blown-up photographs showing her injuries.

"Dr Dunwell's sent these over," he said, enthusiastically. "Come and have a look."

Khan's stomach heaved. The last thing he wanted to start the day with was looking at a battered, blood-stained head. He'd been sickened enough by his glimpses of the body at The Grange. The coloured close-ups were worse!

"Interesting, don't you think?" commented the inspector, passing him the photos. "Tell me, Khan, would *you* have guessed by simply looking at the photos that Miss Bradshaw's killer was left-handed?"

Khan handed them back quickly. "No, sir. I wouldn't."

"Gus Dunwell picked it up immediately once he'd seen the blow-ups. Wonderful thing forensic science, eh, Khan?"

The sergeant nodded. He'd gone noticeably paler.

"It's the angle of the blows on the skull. Here and here. They could only have been struck by someone left-handed." He held the photos up at arm's length to look at them closer. Khan went round on the blind side. "Oh, and he thinks we're looking for a sharp fine-bladed hand-axe. The scalp was cut through clean as a whistle. That's why she bled buckets. See. Here and here."

The inspector thrust the photos under his sergeant's nose.

"Yes," he mused. "These enlargements throw a new dimension on the case."

They brought a whole new dimension to Khan, too. He grimaced and looked away. The inspector gave a satisfied smile and put the prints away. "Now that I've seen these," he said, "I'm going to have another look around The Grange. One or two pieces of the jigsaw are beginning to fall into place at long last. Sergeant Butterworth found some footprints in one of the borders. They were made the day of the murder, but they don't match any we know. Certainly not Woodley's. Too small."

"Fawcett's?" suggested Khan.

"He's even bigger. Shouldn't think they're his."

"I was dining at the Golden Pheasant in Bradford last night," said Khan at last.

"A bit up-market, weren't you," said his boss. "I hear they charge the earth."

Khan ignored him and went straight to the point. "The woman we saw at Grasby Manor was there."

"She who turned you on like a tap? The one with the…well, you know what?"

"The same," grinned Khan. "She came with one of the Quereshis. She's called Jay Hussein."

The inspector gave a soft whistle. "So she's in with the Quereshi lot. I'm not surprised. Go on."

Ibrahim Khan explained what he'd overheard. About her father and the Karachi drug scene. "He's been drug-running over the border with the Afghans for years. Was into it in a big way, sir."

"Was? Not now?" said Hartley.

"He was knocked off not long ago by his suppliers. Upset them somehow. Anyhow, he never came back from his last trip over the border. Disappeared into the blue."

Khan paused, keeping his ace till last.

"Go on," said the inspector. He could see there was more to come.

His sergeant told Blake what the waitress had said. How frightened she was. Then he said, "And one of the guys said Jay Hussein was living with someone right at the top of the Bradford drug-scene. He's got a run all the way from Bradford to Karachi."

"Fawcett!" said the inspector immediately. He saw the look on his sergeant's face and corrected himself quickly. "Then again, it might not be. It don't do to jump to hasty conclusions. Not in our game, Khan."

"You sound just like the Super," said Khan.

Hartley smiled. "Our well blessed lady of fair aspect may have more than one port of call. A woman like her usually has. If I were you, Khan, I'd make another visit to the Golden Pheasant. See if that waitress knows more. You won't look as conspicuous as me visiting the place. I bet she knows a lot more about Jay Hussein than she was prepared to say last night. The Quereshis, too. They'll fit into the picture after what happened to poor Cudworth, I'll be bound. But be careful. Remember you're on the Bradford coppers' pitch. They're a sensitive lot. Give them a tactful buzz first and let them know you're there. Trade a few tit-bits with them before you go in. That'll keep 'em sweet."

Inspector Hartley made for the door and picked up his mac and trilby. He paused before he left to add, "Oh, and while you're about it, call in at forensic and check if Miss Bradshaw's blood is the same as that on the handkerchief found in the kitchen waste-bin. Butterworth is combing the grounds again, now we've some idea what the murder weapon is."

When Blake arrived back at The Grange, the forensic team was searching the gardens again. He asked if they'd found anything new.

"Only the footprints under the window by the study, sir," said Sgt Butterworth. "We've taken casts. The housekeeper says somebody's been lifting saplings newly planted by the gardener there. Thinks it's somebody from the council estate round the corner"

Hartley thanked the sergeant and went in by the main door. It gave him deep satisfaction going in that way. As a boy, he'd once been caught by Fawcett entering by the main door and been ordered back to the tradesmen's entrance. It still rankled.

Like much else about the place, the outside had been neglected. The brass door-handles were green with verdigris The bell-pull was broken. The door was swollen with damp and he had to push hard to open it. When he got inside, there was someone from forensic scraping the carpet where the old lady had fallen.

"Mind if I nose around?" he asked.

"Go ahead, sir," said the other. "I'm almost finished."

"Was it you who found the handkerchief in the bin?" asked Hartley.

"Yes, sir."

"Anything else?"

"Not really, Nothing of importance. The handkerchief had been pushed to the bottom under all the other rubbish. There were bloodstains from it all down the inside."

"Was it a woman's?" asked Hartley

"Yes, sir. Quite an expensive handkerchief, I'd say. Lace round the edge. Looked old. Foreign. They don't have handkerchiefs like that on sale round here," he said, packing up his equipment.

When he'd gone, Hartley stood in the middle of the room. He looked slowly round it, itemising the contents mentally. Antiques cluttered the place. The old lady had had a mania for collecting them and the house was chock full.

The room where she'd died had been her living room for years. She'd rarely left it. She spent the entire day there. Nobody visited except her nephew, and Lizzie Goodwin attended to all her needs.

The furniture was heavy. There were two mahogany military chests and a beautiful walnut chest packed with fine linen, full of table-mats and napkins she never used. An Art Deco bronze and marble mantel clock filled most of a huge mantelpiece, at the end of which was a tall Indian vase.

The detective's eyes moved slowly to the wall opposite where a collection of paintings hung: some water-colours of Dales scenes, an old painting of a farmhouse, a portrait of Miss Bradshaw's grandfather. No mistaking that. He'd the keen hard cast of the rest of them. Mill owners to the core.

An odd assortment of firearms decorated the other walls. Two horse pistols and a Cromwellian breastplate. Beneath it were crossed Civil War handpikes.

The inspector moved behind the chair she'd been in and let his eyes drift round the room again.

There was only one door into the room, directly opposite the chair. Behind the chair were windows in the left and right hand walls. He went across to examine them. No sign of entry there.

"So whoever killed her must have come through the door," he mused. "Her murderer would certainly have been seen by her." His mind began to race and he paced slowly across to her chair speaking to himself.

"If she'd seen whoever it was…coming for her with an axe…she'd have stood up…walked towards them then attempted to defend herself. But she didn't, and she was struck from behind by a blow she didn't expect. Ergo, whoever killed her must have been known to her, and been with her in the room before she died."

He looked again round the room. His eyes came back to the mantelpiece. That vase. He'd seen it somewhere before. It was the same as the one Woodley had been trying to flog to Cudworth! Could that be the reason the old man was beaten up? Had Woodley been systematically robbing his employer and wanted to make sure Cudworth kept quiet?

Hartley hurried across, took out his handkerchief and carefully picked up the heavy vase. The mantelpiece was tall and he had to reach up. He ran his eye along the length of the mantelpiece.

It was thick with dust. What the eye did not see, Lizzie Goodwin's hand didn't dust. There were several rings where the vases had stood. There'd been a pair at one time, moved at intervals, for the rings overlapped where the dust had been disturbed. Why had Woodley stolen only one vase? And why had the vases been constantly moved? Not so that the mantelpiece could be dusted.

He examined the vase carefully before replacing it. It was almost three feet tall with a neck which swept down to a full-bellied base. It had a lid to match. Figures of flying birds and tendrils of leaves stood proud from its sides. A miniature elephant was on the lid. Its base was deep, and the vase free of dust, which Hartley thought strange. The clock was thick with it.

A movement behind him startled the inspector. He turned quickly. There, motionless and smiling, watching him intently, stood Peter Fawcett.

# CHAPTER FIVE

"I should handle that carefully if I were you, Hartley. It's worth a fortune," said Fawcett, advancing into the room.

The inspector recovered and said calmly, "You startled me, sir. Coming in so quietly."

It seemed to please Fawcett, who nodded at the vase. "That's an Indian bronze. Quite rare. Know much about them?"

It was a superfluous question and he knew it. He wanted to show off his expertise to Hartley. He spoke with his old supercilious air, addressing the inspector as he would a servant. By this time he was standing next to him. He picked up the vase and held it at arm's length, turning it round, admiring it. Then he replaced it and faced the inspector, looking at him closely.

"I'm not into antiques, sir, " said Hartley. He felt angry he'd let himself be caught unawares. Even more angry as old feelings of inferiority swept back.

"It's one of a pair," explained Fawcett. "There was another but my aunt must have sold it. She fancied herself as a dealer."

"Did she have an outlet? An agent?" asked Hartley.

"The antiques shop in Chatsworth Street took much of her stuff. They did well out of her. She'd no idea really how much her antiques were worth. She always bought them cheap at sales. It became her only interest before she became housebound. A fixation almost. She bought at random. The house is chocker with them. Some have become quite valuable over the years."

He spoke with a slight drawl. An affectation Blake Hartley remembered from old. He'd never liked it. Donaldson had it, too.

"She certainly had an eye for the unusual," commented the inspector, for something to say. "Like the vase…and those weapons on the wall."

"She was a magpie collector, not a connoisseur," said Fawcett sharply. "I've inherited her flair for antiques, but not her taste, thank God. At the same time, I wouldn't mind having that vase. It was one of her better purchases." He looked at the vase again thoughtfully. Then he said, "Dreadful to think of auntie snuffing it the way she did. Dreadful! I can't get over it."

"Murder's a cardinal sin," said Hartley, eyeing him intently.

"Oh, yes. I was forgetting. You're very much into religion aren't you, Hartley. Always were if I remember rightly. And now you're one of these new-fangled priests. What do you call yourselves?" said Fawcett with more than a hint of mockery.

"Non-stipendiary ministers, sir," Hartley heard himself saying humbly.

"Non-stipendiary magistrates I've heard of, but not non-stipendiary priests!" said the other with a laugh.

"We earn our keep working in the secular world," said Hartley doggedly. But he knew he wasn't being taken seriously. His words were falling on a hard heart if not deaf ears.

"Worker priests and all that. Good for you, Hartley. You were always a good worker. But I'm afraid religion isn't my forte. I suppose I'm a lapsed Anglican. Very lapsed. But fancy you, a policeman-priest!" He laughed again. He found the notion amusing. But the inspector simply smiled back. He'd been well used to having his leg pulled over his priesthood at first, till his colleagues began to take him seriously when they turned to him for help and advice. They didn't pull his leg now.

Fawcett looked him over patronisingly. "I must say you've done well for yourself, though. Your mother would have been proud of you. She always was. Always telling my aunt how well you were doing at school and later. An Anglican priest and an English police-inspector all rolled into one. That's quite an achievement!"

"You might call it that," said the inspector. "I'd say it's just the way things have worked out."

Fawcett ignored his remark. "Mind if I smoke, old fellow?" he asked, pulling out a silver cigarette case. The 'old fellow' bit sounded like a concession, but he didn't wait for a reply. He took a black gold-tipped Turkish cigarette from his case and lit up, inhaling deeply.

Neither spoke for a moment. Then Inspector Hartley said, "It seems strange meeting again, sir, after all those years. We both spent our youth here."

"Yes. Almost like the old days…except this was never your home, was it? Not like it was mine. I loved the old place when I was a boy. Couldn't get away from school fast enough to return here. Beastly place, school. This was the only real home I ever had."

The wistful tone in Fawcett's voice surprised the inspector. "You're right, sir. This was never my home," he said, warmly. "Coming here from Garlic Lane was like entering another world."

It was Fawcett's turn to be stumped for a reply. He gave his boyish laugh and strolled to the French windows. The view from that side of the house was still attractive, despite the peeping-tom roofs of the council houses looking over the boundary wall.

Immediately below the windows there were flower-beds running along a gravel path. That, in turn, followed a grassy bank dropping to the lawns. At the end of the lawns was a broad flight of steps, guarded by two flower vases held aloft by nymphs. Then the ground fell away further to a rose-garden and the hedge which hid the vegetable plots.

In the old days, the vegetable garden had reached right up to the boundary wall, beyond which there had used to be a meadow. It was filled with houses now. Where the drive had entered the meadow stood a pair of lodge cottages. Sammy Woodley and Lizzie Goodwin lived in them now. Their cottages marked the end of the drive and beyond was the council estate. The big wrought-iron gates across the drive between the cottages were permanently locked

"Not much has changed here since we were young, eh?" observed Fawcett, gazing dreamily through the windows. "Only the world about us. Pity we have to grow up."

"Change is inevitable," said the inspector. He realised he sounded banal, but he didn't think Fawcett had changed all that much. He still had the same supercilious air he'd had years before.

Fawcett countered with, "Plus ça change, plus c'est la même chose."

"Aye," said Hartley. "'And there is nothing new under the sun as the old preacher said."

Fawcett seemed surprised by Hartley's knowledge. He gave another of his laughs and drew on his cigarette. "But it really was a beautiful place in which to grow up. If only I could have appreciated it then as I do now. I like it more the older I grow. I like all old things which are beautiful. More and more. I suppose I'm clinging to the past. An age of innocence, Hartley."

Why, he didn't know, but just at that moment Hartley genuinely felt empathy with him. Just for a moment he, too, yearned for the past they'd both shared.

"The past becomes more precious, more golden with age," Fawcett continued, speaking as much to himself as to the inspector and breaking the silence which had settled again. "I suppose that's why I returned to these parts after living abroad for years. It may surprise you, Hartley, but I love the old town and the moors around it. It's my past. I'm part of it, just as it's part of me." And Hartley couldn't help agreeing with him.

While he spoke, Fawcett looked out of the window. He ran his eye along the line of beech trees at the end of the lawn; then to the border beneath where they stood. There were gaps in the hedge which was newly planted..

A frown crossed his face and he said irritably, "Some blighter's been lifting the new hedge Woodley planted. It's the people from the council estate, y'know. My aunt had no end of trouble with them." It was ironic that Fawcett with his shady past should get so het up about a few saplings being stolen.

"So you have trouble with folk from the estate?" asked Hartley.

"Damned nuisances. Know no different, I suppose. The old are as bad as the young. Born thieves the lot of 'em," he said. "But I suppose it keeps you people in business."

"We're the only ones crime pays, sir," quipped Hartley with the ghost of a smile.

"You're quite a comical old card beneath that dour exterior, Hartley," said Fawcett. "Quite a card. I can see what your superintendent means when he says you have a droll sense of humour. We play golf together, y'know. He's often spoken about you." Then he paused. "He says you're no nearer solving my aunt's murder. Are you?"

The directness of his question surprised Hartley. He thought it a cheek, but all he said was, "You might say that, sir. Whoever did it certainly covered his tracks well."

A smile flickered across the other's face. "Well, I hope you soon catch him. He's a dangerous psychopath whoever he is. Battering a helpless old woman to death."

"What makes you think he's a man who murdered your aunt, sir?" asked the inspector.

Fawcett shrugged his shoulders. "Can't imagine a woman doing anything as terrible as this."

"Then you don't know women," said the inspector.

The other shot him a quick glance, unsure of what he was driving at. He said lamely, "Well, whoever did it, I hope they're soon caught."

Suddenly he ran out of steam; as if he'd tired of playing his game. He looked at his watch. "Good Lord! Is that the time?" he said. "I'm late as it is. If you'll excuse me, inspector, I must be off. It's been nice meeting you again. We've had quite a jolly chat."

He turned to go, but Hartley halted him with, "Before you go, sir, I'd be grateful if you'd jot down a few details about this vase. I'm very taken with it."

"Of course, old fellow," said Fawcett. He took out his pen and jotted down some notes on the paper Hartley gave him. The inspector noticed he wrote left-handed, which was strange. He used his right hand for most other things like lighting his cigarette or holding the vase. "Cost you a packet if you wanted to buy it," he said, putting his pen away. "A couple of grand at least."

"A bit out of my bracket, but I just thought I'd ask," said Hartley.

Fawcett hung on a moment, as if expecting Hartley to elaborate why the vase appealed so much. But the inspector said nothing. As the other left, the inspector commented on the beautiful place Fawcett had at Grasby.

"I'm glad you like it. You must come again - and bring your sergeant with you. I'm sure he'd like to have a closer look at my collection of furniture," Fawcett replied, pausing in the doorway.

"That's kind of you, sir. We may well take you up on that. Doubtless we'll have one or two more routine questions to ask about the case here, and it'll be a nice place to ask 'em," said Hartley and wished him good-day as he left.

When he'd gone, Blake Hartley moved to the window overlooking the drive. The vintage Alvis was there. Fawcett had replaced the original wheels and tyres with new more souped-up ones. He slammed the car into gear and it took off, screeching out of the drive. He paused a moment at the gate before roaring into Keighworth. The inspector could hear him all the way into town.

Then Hartley strolled back to the mantelpiece and took a long hard look at the bronze vase. He stood on tip-toe to confirm where its partner had been. Satisfied, he left the house for the council estate. He was curious about who'd nicked the saplings. Whoever had done that might be able to tell him something else.

# CHAPTER SIX

To reach the estate, he had to pass the cottages where the housekeeper and gardener lived. Lizzie Goodwin came to her door. She'd watched him come all the way down the drive.

There was no greeting. "Did t'police find owt fresh?" she asked bluntly, and kept wiping her hands nervously on her pinafore.

"Aye, Lizzie," he said. "We'll catch whoever's done it. Be sure of that. We've found a handkerchief in the kitchen bin. Stuffed underneath all the rubbish. It had blood on it. Know owt about it?"

Her face tightened and she wiped her hands faster.

"What sort of hankie?" she asked guardedly.

"A fancy one. Expensive. The sort Miss Bradshaw had," replied the inspector.

"Aye. She had expensive hankies all right. Lace an' all. She'd got drawers full of 'em. Fancy stuff she brought back from abroad when she were younger. Hankies, linen tablecloths, napkins - you name it. She never used half of 'em. And she never gave owt away!"

"When you go up to the house, have a look at it. The sergeant has it. Tell him I sent you. Confirm it's hers," said Hartley.

She stopped wiping her hands and folded them under her pinnie. She began looking at him in an odd, half-witted way which disturbed him. He switched to the missing trees. Had she noticed anyone on the estate planting a new hedge? She frequently crossed the estate to visit a friend.

She was relieved he'd stopped asking about the handkerchief. That was obvious. She threw a suspicious glance over her shoulder and asked him to step inside. "It don't do to talk out here," she said. "I don't want to be seen talking to thee. Tongues wag, round here." She nodded in the direction of the estate through the gates.

He followed her in and glanced round her kitchen. It matched her housekeeping at The Grange. It was dusty and cluttered. Cheap prints hung on one wall alongside a row of plaster ducks flying ceilingwards. On another wall were faded family photos. Some from her childhood on the farm in the east of the county. Among them was a portrait of herself as a young woman. Blake was struck how handsome she'd once been. He'd forgotten that. She turned and faced him when she'd closed the door. She didn't ask him to sit or offer him tea. It was obvious she wanted him out as quickly as possible.

"There's a chap called Roe on Meadow Avenue. A right shifty 'un. He's allus hanging about seeing what he can pick up. Sammy's caught him in t'grounds before an' once gave him a good hiding, but he still sneaks back. I told Miss Bradshaw to report him to t'police, but she took no notice. She never listened to me. She's allus treated me an' Sammy like muck."

It opened a catalogue of tales about her being treated like muck, which the inspector had to endure. When she'd done, Hartley asked if she'd access to Sammy Woodley's cottage.

"As housekeeper I've all the spare keys," she said proudly. She pointed to a row of keys hanging near the door.

"If he doesn't come back soon, I'll have to look round his place," said the inspector.

Lizzie frowned. "What does tha want to go poking round there for? There's nowt there worth looking at," she said.

"This is a murder inquiry, Lizzie," he replied patiently. "I've got to check everything out. Including Sammy Woodley. I'm surprised he isn't here."

"He's got a lady friend in Skiproyd," she said, lowering her voice. "He visits her on his days off. But he's always back the next day in a general way. If he were late, Miss Bradshaw grumbled like mad. She were allus grumbling at us. Had tantrums at times. We were muck under her feet!"

Hartley took his leave. She'd nothing good to say about her late mistress although she'd kept her employed after all the other servants had left. Nobody else would. She almost seemed pleased her employer was dead. She showed no signs of grief or loss. She stood at the door when he'd gone, watching him take the side-gate into the estate. Then she went up to The Grange.

The council estate was run down. Thrown up between the wars, the cheap houses were pebble-dashed and bore ugly scars where the rendering had come away and been patched up. Most needed a new coat of paint, except one. The house of the hedge-swiper stood out like a beacon on that drab estate.

Wilf Roe was a do-it-yourself freak. He'd an abundance of enthusiasm but few skills. At some time he'd acquired a job lot of cheap brilliantly red paint which he'd slapped on everywhere: window frames, front door, back door, garden fence - the lot! His house hit you as soon as you turned into the avenue.

His garden was just as bizarre. It contained an amazing collection of plastic gnomes in a variety of poses sitting on plastic toadstools by little plastic windmills. Strings of rancid bacon rind hung from three bird-tables round a tiny pond into which another plastic gnome with a fishing rod gazed soulfully. The pond was by a retaining wall at the bottom of his garden. Above it, behind the low red fence, was a row of newly planted beech saplings!

Inspector Hartley opened the red gate with some difficulty and walked slowly up the path. Yet another garish ornament made from sea-shells stood by the door. The door opened slowly and suspiciously and he showed his ID to a small weasel-faced man, who couldn't look him in the eye. When he saw the inspector's ID the man turned pale. For a moment, Hartley thought he was going to slam the door in his face and bolt, but he opened the door wider and stepped back, glancing over his shoulder.

"Yer've come about that hedge, haven't yer?" he croaked. "I can explain everything, boss. Honest I can."

Hartley said he knew all about the hedge, but he'd come about something more important - Miss Bradshaw's murder. "You were seen leaving her garden the night she was killed. That's what I want to question you about. Don't you think we ought to go where we can talk in private?"

"Aye," said the other, and began to look as if he could throw up any minute.

Blake entered the house and Roe did his best to close the door quietly behind him. But someone upstairs had been listening intently and a woman's strident voice yelled out, "Who the hell is it, Wilf, at this time o' day? If it's t'milkman come for his money, tell him I'll be down in a minute. I've nearly done."

"It's not t'milkman, luv," Wilf shouted back grimly. "It's police. They've come about t'murder up at big house."

A pause. Then a lavatory flushed. "Hang on! I'll be right down!" shouted the voice again from upstairs as its owner made herself decent.

Hartley knew he hadn't much time to speak with Roe before the voice came down and took over. The weasel-faced man confirmed he was Wilfred Roe and when the inspector asked what he was doing in the grounds of The Grange the night Miss Bradshaw was murdered, Roe ran his fingers nervously through his hair..

He took out a grubby tin of tobacco and some roll-ups from his coat pocket then lit up. Yes, he'd been nicking saplings for his garden hedge. He was hard up, on benefits and had been for years since he'd had to stop work with a bad chest. His wife didn't get much though she worked on the till at Readimart. They were buying their house from the council, so he couldn't afford to buy his hedge. He couldn't let his wife pay for everything. Then he fell into a despairing silence and puffed heavily on his fag as heavy footsteps came downstairs.

The room seemed full when Mrs Roe entered and stood by the window. She was huge. Twice the size of her husband with a face like an angry Rottweiler. She was ready to tackle anyone, including Blake Hartley. The inspector introduced himself and she glared first at her husband, who fell silent, then at Hartley.

She'd a voice to match her face and it came at you non-stop.. "I were only saying to my Wilf before you came, inspector, it's hardly real. You can't sleep safe in your beds these days, can you? You just can't take it in when summat like this happens on your own doorstep. I meantersay, you read it in t'papers every day and see it on t'telly, but it doesn't seem real till it happens to you, does it? You can't fathom it, can you?. Poor Miss Bradshaw. She might have had her faults and we all knew about them. But we all have faults, don't we? She didn't deserve that though, did she? Nobody deserves that. I meantersay..."

She meant to say a great deal more, but Hartley cut in, stopping her in full flow. He'd like to speak to her husband - alone. She looked put out. Her mouth opened slightly in a pout, but she took the hint and left to make some tea. Hartley heard her pottering about in the kitchen for a moment. Then there was silence and her shadow appeared just outside the door after she'd put the kettle on. It disappeared when the inspector stood up and pushed the door to slightly.

"Mr Roe," said the inspector when he'd resumed his seat, "cast your mind back and think very carefully. The night Miss Bradshaw was murdered, did you see or hear anything unusual when you were nicking those trees? Tell me all you know and we might forget about the hedge."

Roe took a deep pull on his fag. "Let me see," he said screwing up his eyes. "It would be just after eight when I went there. It gets dark about half-seven and I waited till Woodley had pushed off. He goes out Tuesdays and don't come back till late on Wednesday. Anyway, when I saw him leave his cottage an' Mrs Goodwin go to bingo, I nipped through t'gates."

"You keep your tabs on those two pretty well," observed Hartley.

"I have to. I got roughed up by Woodley once. And when Lizzie Goodwin gets her knife into yer, she never stops. Shouts at yer in t'middle of town. She don't care what she says or who's there. She's a right devil."

The inspector was learning much. He checked Roe's timings and asked again if he'd seen anything unusual.

"Aye… Woodley," he said. "He hadn't gone. He were still there. I'd just got up to t'big house when out he comes wi' another bloke who spoke lah-di-dah. I couldn't see either of 'em but I heard 'em all right, and I'd recognise Woodley's voice anywhere. I stayed hidden against t'wall. I dared scarcely breathe I was so shit-scared."

"What did they say?"

"Summat about Woodley taking care of a vase when he went to Skiproyd. I couldn't make it out. But t'chap wi' t'posh voice told him to be extra careful. Then Woodley pushed off and t'other went inside. As soon as they'd gone, I bloody scarpered, I can tell yer. I were so scared I left me spade behind and had to go back for it later."

"What time was that?" asked Hartley.

"About ten. Lizzie came back from bingo and I damned near collided wi' her when I went to pick it up. It just weren't my night, boss," he said wryly.

He fell silent as his wife wheezed in and plonked a tray with tea and biscuits before them. She wanted to hear more and stayed on glaring from one to the other, but she was disappointed.. There was no more to say. Hartley had learned all he wanted and drank his cup of tea. Then he thanked them and left before Mrs Roe began meantersaying again.

He raised his trilby to her when she followed him out, standing at the door arms akimbo, her husband peering round her. Then, having closed the garish gate, Blake hummed quietly to himself and strolled up the avenue back to The Grange. Things at last were beginning to fall into place.

# CHAPTER SEVEN

While Inspector Hartley was at The Grange, Sergeant Khan went to Bradford, doing a bit of sleuthing to find out more about Jay Hussein and Quereshi. The waitress at the tandoori gave him the name of a pub in a seedy part of town. Very seedy! The Old Ram. He didn't take his boss's advice and contact the drugs squad in Bradford. He was too like Hartley and his mistake almost proved his undoing.

He was brought up in Bradford but had rarely visited the area round the Old Ram. It was dog-rough then. Wearing an old pair of torn jeans and a dirty donkey jacket, Ibrahim Khan took a deep breath and turned off the main road into Beckett Street. At the end of it stood the Old Ram.

He had a long slummy walk ahead of him and a cul-de-sac at the end. There was no way out once he was in. Anyone going down it had to face the gauntlet of the residents. And a mucky lot they were.

The further he walked down it, the filthier grew the street. Garbage spilled from the broken-down yards on to the sidewalk and into the road. Half-way down a pack of mangy dogs harassed a bitch on heat. She turned and snapped as they tried to mount, before scurrying into a backyard. A fat woman came out with a pan full of water and flung it over the randy pack. They scattered, then re-grouped, hanging about the gate sniffing and snapping.

Gum-chewing thugs lounged outside one house and eyed Khan suspiciously. Nearer the pub, hookers hawked their wares. On some waste ground next to the pub four junkies sat looking into space. And in the entry between the pub and a row of houses someone was pissing against the wall. The street stank of stale urine and sewage.

After what seemed an age, Khan reached the pub. More than once he'd been tempted to turn back, but his curiosity led him on. His gut felt like a tight knot by the time he reached the pub and hesitated outside the door. A huge Caribbean Brit with greasy dreadlocks was just coming out. He noticed Khan's hesitation and asked him what he wanted.

"I -I want some sensi," whispered Khan, licking his lips nervously. "I was told to come here."

The other looked at him, hard. Satisfied he said, "Ain't got no sensi, man. I can sell you hash. Real fine hash."

Khan pulled out a fiver. "Will this do?"

The other snatched it from him. "Sure, man. Come inside."

"Sure there's no coppers in there?" asked Khan naively.

The other laughed. "Pigs! Give me a break. We eat 'em for breakfast in there! You're OK with me, man. But stick close. There's some real mean folks in there. Don't do to walk in without an intro."

One of the junkies lurched across and began laughing crazily. He pulled out a knife and began demanding a fix. The black man grabbed his wrist, twisted it, and the knife fell harmlessly to the ground. As the junkie stopped to retrieve it, the other stood on his hand and pressed heavily. The junkie screamed with pain, and left the knife on the ground when the black man released his boot.

"See what I mean, man?" he said to Khan. "And he's nothin' compared with what's in there!"

As they entered the pub he asked where Khan was from. Who'd told him about the Old Ram?.

The sergeant said he'd come in from Burnley with his father. They dealt in fent-ends throughout Lancashire and had come to buy stock from a warehouse. It was the first time he'd been to Bradford with his dad and he'd been there all morning and badly needed a smoke. He'd been told by some guy who worked in the warehouse where to go. While his dad was eating, he'd come to the Old Ram.

The other nodded. "Follow me. But like I said, stick close. You keep your eyes fixed on me and don't look round. OK, man?"

The pub was almost as dirty as the street outside. The sickly sweet smell of cannabis mingled with the stench of stale ale. The place was packed with junkies and their suppliers. Many smoked roll-ups. Some just stared into space as high as skylarks. A group watched horse-racing on the telly at one end of the room. From another room came the familiar click of snooker balls.

They went to the bar and Khan ordered drinks. Dreadlocks never left his side. When they got to a table, the black man pulled out a small packet of cannabis, gave it to Khan and watched him roll a reefer. Khan had practised hard rolling cigarettes before leaving Keighworth. He'd never smoked in his life, nor did he drink being a devout Muslim. Only when he had to in the fight against crime. Hartley had sometimes been in the same boat and had helped him there. Crime was evil and in their fight against it both sometimes had had to compromise their religious beliefs. If the devil could subvert their religion with hypocrisy, they could fight him with his own weapon.

The sergeant sipped his beer gingerly. Then he lit up. The first pull nearly choked him, but somehow he held on. He'd drunk a bottle of milk before leaving home. Hartley had taught him that trick. So the alcohol didn't take effect at once.

But cannabis was another matter. His head began to ache. He felt sick and found it difficult to concentrate and ask the right questions. As it was, Dreadlocks did most of the talking. Asking his name. His voice seemed a long way off.

"Mohtar Mohammed," he heard himself saying. "What's yours?"

"Ain't got no name, man. Call me Crack. Everyone else does," he laughed loudly. Then asked, "Like it?"

Khan was befuddled. He didn't know whether he was referring to his name or the joint he was smoking. He went for the latter.

"Good stuff," he said, feigning enjoyment.

"The best, man. All the way from Morocco," said Crack. He laughed again and those near him laughed with him. It was some in-joke lost on Khan. In fact, the whole of life was rapidly becoming lost on him.Folk began to move and speak in slow-motion. Colour and noise became intense. Unbearable. He stopped smoking and took a sip of beer. Anything to clear his mouth. He focussed his eyes on the other side of the room and suddenly, through the haze, he saw Abdul Quereshi.

He was carrying a briefcase and a large hold-all. He looked in a hurry. He went straight to the bar and handed his case to the barman, who opened it and checked something inside. Satisfied, he snapped the case shut and took it away. When he came back he had a large vase - identical with the one Woodley had given to Cudworth! Quereshi shoved it quickly into his hold-all then left, nodding at one or two acquaintances. It all happened so quickly, Sergeant Khan in his befuddled state could barely take it in.

Sgt Khan turned away for Quereshi had to pass him on the way out. The way the rest of the pub treated him made it clear he had clout. When he'd gone he asked Crack who he was. The other shrugged his shoulders. "He's known as Q. Like I'm Crack," was all he said. "Don't ask no questions, man, and forget you ever seen him. OK?"

Khan nodded and the room spun even more.

"He's bad news if you cross him. Runs for the Big White Chief. The boss-man. The big boss right at the top. OK?"

By now Khan's head felt the size of a football filled with lead. He said he had to go and got unsteadily to his feet thanking Crack for the joint.

"Any time, man," said Crack. "But always ask for Crack first. Safer that way. Lucky you met me, man."

Khan shook his hand. "Lucky I did," he said and made for the door.

The room moved with him. Crack's features went fish-eye and his grin threatened to split his face. Ibrahim Khan wiped his eyes and clutched at the table. He collided with someone seated at a table, and immediately the guy stood up and took a swing at Khan.

Crack stepped in and pushed the other to his seat. "Easy, man. Easy," he said. "You gonna lose me a real cool customer." Crack was big and powerful, a black Hercules, and the other sat quiet. "Sorry about that, Mohtar. He's blown," he said to Khan. "But you'd better go. Quick!"

Ibrahim staggered through the door. He could mix it with the best when sober. But he was high and he was drunk. He lurched down the street and as he reached the gang half-way down, they began to tail him, sensing an easy mugging.

He just had to stop, he felt so rotten. As he turned the yobbos moved towards him. He pulled a knife and lunged at them and made them back off. Then he turned to the wall and threw up. Somewhere high above him a woman's voice screeched from a window telling him to fuck off. So he slewed on again till he reached the main road.

There he leaned against the wall stupidly watching the traffic go by, barely aware that a police-car had drawn up. He reeled as two cops got out and began frisking him. They found what they wanted: the packet Crack had sold him. Then they began firing questions. He found that amusing and began giggling.

Meanwhile, the gang which had tailed him formed a tight hostile ring round him and the police. They began shouting obscenities. "Get him into the car," said one of the officers quickly, and opened the door. Khan felt his arm being shoved up his back and he was bundled into the car with a cop beside him. The other got into the driving seat.

Ibrahim Khan kept trying to say who he was, but he didn't make sense. Anyhow, nobody would listen. The yobbos began banging on the side of the car which sped off. Then Khan threw up again and shortly after passed out. When he came to, he was in a police cell.

# CHAPTER EIGHT

The atmosphere in Keighworth Police Station next day was brittle. Something was about to snap. When Ibrahim Khan had recovered sufficiently to tell the Bradford Police who he was, there followed a long one-sided telephone conversation in which Detective Chief Superintendent Peters of the Bradford Met let Donaldson know exactly what he thought of the Keighworth CID, what he thought of Donaldson's sergeant being found stoned in a red-light district, and finally what he thought of Donaldson himself.

It didn't go down well. Donaldson hated eating humble pie and he'd had to take it all. He was the least experienced superintendent in the county. He'd been still wet behind the ears when he'd arrived in Keighworth a few years previously, full of paper qualifications and college courses. "Full of vaulting ambition," Hartley had said - and he was being polite. Donaldson was full of whom he knew and, most of all, he was full of himself. Now he was full of humble pie.

He'd been ruthless in his climb to the top, accelerated by licking many pairs of boots of people in high places. His had been a meteoric rise strewn with the careers of colleagues he'd used then abandoned. No way did he want that rise halted now by a bull-headed, muddling, out-of-date inspector and a foolish sergeant.

He had Hartley hauled in first thing and carpeted Khan when he arrived later. Blake was baffled when the duty sergeant said he was to go straight to Arthur Donaldson's office. He'd no idea what was up. He thought it must be something to do with the way he organised his office. Donaldson was always on about his lack of routine, his chronic untidiness.

Shortly after his appointment, Donaldson had button-holed the inspector and told him that a man's office was a reflection of the man himself. "A tidy well-run office reveals a tidy, well-run mind," he'd said, for he kept his own office immaculate. He was neurotic about it.

When he walked into Hartley's office the first time he pontificated, "An office tells you everything about a man, inspector. Especially his desk," he'd said, with a withering glance at the chaos on Hartley's desk. "You really ought to keep your office a little more tidy."

It was littered with tea-cups, papers and poetry books. The inspector was always reading. Donaldson rarely read fiction and never poetry. There wasn't a line of verse in him and no imagination. He complained about the inconsequential reading matter on view and said Hartley must get rid of it at once. Had he opened Hartley's drawers he'd have discovered a whole library of books - and the odd sermon!

In contrast, his own office was so regimented, he brought it to attention whenever he entered. All was spick and span. All in place. There was nothing on his desk except a pen, a pencil (newly sharpened each day) his notepad and a masonic paperweight. They were moved at intervals during the day; but at the end they all went back in place: the pen, the pencil, the notepad and the paperweight.

When he'd said years ago that a desk revealed the mind of the person behind it, Hartley had replied ingenuously, "I agree, sir. If there's a lot on a desk, there must be a lot in the mind of the man behind it." Donaldson had no reply. He sensed he was being got at, but couldn't fathom how.

His own office trumpeted his ego. He'd been an oarsman at college and a rowing-oar with a light-blue blade with his Cambridge days proclaimed it. It bore his name in gold letters picked out from the rest of the crew and hung on the wall behind his chair.

It was the first thing you saw as you entered the room. The next was the shelf of trophies he'd picked up playing golf. The paperweight was designed to impress, too. That had pride of place on his desk, for the Super was an ardent freemason. The golf-club and the Masonic Lodge were his sole interests outside work. Oh, and he was a Reader, too, at a smart church in Ilkesworth, where he lived, though he didn't do any theological reading now.

Ties were another of his trumpetings. He wore only three: his old school tie (a minor public school called Axchester); his Cambridge college tie; and a more recent one, the Royal Ridings Golf Club tie. He was especially proud of that.

When Inspector Hartley entered the superintendent's office, Donaldson went for him at once, keeping him standing in front of his desk throughout the interview while he paced angrily backwards and forwards the other side.

"Why the hell didn't you order Khan to inform the Bradford force before he went blundering into their patch?" he barked. "I should have thought that was common-sense…of which, it seems, there's a singular lack in your office, Hartley! And what was he doing carrying cannabis? Why was he there at all? Why wasn't I told? It's me who's carrying the can now, Hartley. But, by God, you two are going to hold it soon. And it's red-hot, believe me! You're supposed to be conducting a murder inquiry, Hartley. Not peddling drugs!"

"I'd a hunch…" began the inspector, but he was cut short.

"We don't act on hunches here, inspector," said the Super. "Cold hard facts are what we work with. Proven data. Good God, man, you ought to know that by now! Anything less and we're laughed out of court."

He'd worked himself up into a right old lather and went to the window to collect himself. Then he stoked up again.

"By God, Hartley, you're heading for the mother and father of a cock-up if you're relying on hunches. We've got Fawcett looking over our shoulders the whole time in this case. And he has clout. Clout in the very highest places. One false move and you'll have the whole damned establishment on us like a ton of bricks, the Chief Constable included, and I don't want his noose put round my neck!"

Then he had to elaborate, telling the inspector that Fawcett had been at his old college in Cambridge, who he'd played golf with at the Royal Ridings, the Deputy Lord Lieutenant, Sir Henry Locke and His Honour Judge Laybank - all personal friends of Fawcett. Any one of them could finish his career.

Blake Hartley listened dutifully. He'd heard it all before. And as he ranted on, Blake mused how such a silly little twerp had risen so far so fast in the force. When he was Donaldson's age, you got on through sheer slog. Starting at the bottom on the beat. No paperwork and few courses then.

But then Donaldson had contacts. For starters he was a public school man and a bishop's son. His wife also came from an upper-class background, too. He'd a social studies degree from Cambridge and claimed he'd done some hush-hush work there for Special Branch. When he left, he did some lecturing on sociology at the Police College, as a civilian. Then he entered the force - in traffic control. After a spell in the Home Counties, he came north.

When he arrived in Keighworth, he'd turned the place upside down and added layer on layer of bureaucracy. New procedures, new lines of communication (all done by pigeon-hole), new staff structures, were all put in place. The station didn't know whether it was coming or going. Neither did Donaldson.

Blake Hartley and Ibrahim Khan had been the first casualties. They'd been passed over time and time again for promotion, while younger less experienced but more socio-literate and vocal colleagues went up the league tables ahead of them. In time, Donaldson had built up his own cosy coterie of boot-lickers at the station, most of them freemasons like himself. Hartley and Khan were not among them.

Inspector Hartley listened patiently that morning till his boss ran out of steam, "By God, Hartley, if Sir William gets to hear of this we can all say goodbye to promotion. Good job Chief Superintendent Peters is in my Lodge, else we'd be up to our necks. He's promised it won't go any further."

Hartley gave his boss a wry look.

"I know you don't altogether agree with Masonry, Hartley, but this time it's saved your bacon. At least we Masons are loyal to each other. Which is more than I can say for some folks."

Another wry look from the inspector.

"Remember you have Peters to thank for that. I don't know why, but he's got a soft spot for you. For God's sake don't let it happen again."

Donaldson paused and stared out of the window. Inspector Hartley stayed silent. After some moments, his boss turned. He didn't like silence. It oppressed him. The medallions on his watch chain jingled as he turned.

"Well," he barked. "Have you nothing to say?"

This time a righteous, accusing look on Hartley's face. "Only this, sir. I'd be grateful if you'd stop taking God's name in vain. I'd rather you didn't use the Almighty's name so freely, sir. You being a Reader and all that."

The Super swelled visibly and went red in the face as he struggled with his temper. "From anyone else I'd have regarded that as impertinence!" he hissed.

Hartley looked hurt. "It's a matter of principle, sir. Not impertinence. May I go now?"

Donaldson could only nod at the door and Hartley left.

When Khan came in he looked washed out, hung over. The inspector was reading John Donne's sermons, to calm down after the roasting his boss had given him.

"Oh, I wondered when you were going to put in an appearance," he said wearily. "I don't rightly know what's happened, but I've been given a proper pasting by our Arthur. He's still gibbering about you and the Bradford lot."

Khan crept to his desk and put his head in his hands.

"You look as though you need a cuppa, son," said Hartley, nodding in the direction of the tea-tray. "Ramadan or not, you'd better get something inside you before you go up to our Arthur. He wants your guts for garters. Now tell me all about it. I'd no idea what he was wittering on about."

"I'm sorry, sir," began Khan. "I really am sorry, landing you in it. But

I did get a lead, sir."

Hartley brightened. "Oh?"

"I went into a pub which pushed drugs and Abdul Quereshi came in. He's pushing in a big way."

"Surprise, surprise," said Hartley. "And?"

"He had a vase there exactly like the one Woodley gave Cudworth in Skipworth," said Khan, and went on to relate all that had happened and how Quereshi had carefully checked the bottom of the vase.

"Checked the bottom of the vase, did he?" said Hartley thoughtfully when his sergeant had done. "Did you tell that to the Bradford lot?"

Khan grimaced. "I only just about convinced them who I was before they threw me out," he said.

"You'd better go up and face our Arthur. He's champing at the bit," said the inspector gloomily. "It's bad enough when he's wrong. But when he's right it's twice as nasty."

When Khan left, he picked up the book he'd been reading and smiled to himself as he read the title: "That by Discord things get Better."

# CHAPTER NINE

It was becoming clear why Fawcett had put in that surprise visit at The Grange. Inspector Hartley had no proof, but he was now convinced Fawcett was running a drugs racket. If Donaldson had known what was going on in his inspector's mind, he'd have taken him off the case immediately! In addition, Hartley felt Fawcett was linked to his aunt's murder. Intuition and a growing sense of orderliness about the whole business led him to that conclusion.

Like Donaldson's desk, everything about the case was too neat. There was no clue at all who'd killed the old woman, except a first-class mind behind the whole affair. Fawcett certainly had that. And after what Khan had told him, the inspector guessed Fawcett had come back for the vase before the police got hold of it. It was sheer chance Hartley had got there just before him. To walk in and find him holding the very thing he wanted must have shaken Fawcett rigid.

While Khan was being mauled by their boss about the screwed up trip to Bradford, Hartley hurried back to The Grange, hoping against hope Fawcett hadn't been there again. He just had to check out the base of the vase now. He screeched to a halt outside the front door and hurried into the lounge. He flung open the door and sighed with relief. The vase was still where he'd left it.

Walking across, he gingerly lifted it on to the table. Then he tried unscrewing the base. Nothing happened at first then slowly it started to move. It was stiff and he redoubled his efforts, going red in the face.

It took him some moments then suddenly it came away. He looked inside and carefully scraped away some traces of white powder still left inside onto a filter paper. That done, he screwed back the base, wiped the outside and replaced it on the mantelpiece. The filter paper he pocketed.

"Softly, softly, catchee monkey by the tail," he murmured, mopping his brow. "And if we catch the monkey Fawcett with that, we'll have more than his tail."

He was about to leave when he heard someone chopping wood not far away. He was curious and moved to the side of the window. Outside her cottage, Lizzie Goodwin was chopping wood. She broke off to fan a garden fire and get it blazing. Then she began chopping again. He watched her unobserved for a while, then decided to visit her. She seemed mighty keen to burn whatever was on her fire.

She'd gone inside with her wood by the time he arrived. He hurried to the fire and looked closely at it. She was burning more than garden rubbish on it. The pungent smell of rubber had met him all down the drive.

There was a pair of slippers burning fiercely and what looked like a leather wallet. He thought it odd. Why should she go to the trouble of burning them when she could just have easily dumped them in the waste-bin?

While she was inside, he poked the remains of the wallet clear. Something had caught his eye. Some initials in gold lettering - "E.M.B." Miss Bradshaw's. He quickly extinguished the smouldering leather, then wrapped it in his hankie. A moment later, Lizzie re-appeared.

She was taken aback to see him by the fire. Annoyed, too, by her heavy scowl. "What does tha want?" she growled, eyeing him suspiciously. "Ah thowt tha'd finished 'ere."

"Oh, no. Not for some time, Lizzie," he answered. "Not till we've found Miss Bradshaw's killer."

Lizzie stood sullen. When she began poking the fire vigorously he asked what she was burning. She continued poking the fire and said she was clearing things out. She might have to leave. A new owner wouldn't want to keep her on. "But Mr Fawcett is the new owner. I'm sure he won't turn you out. He was always kind to you," said Hartley.

As soon as he mentioned Fawcett's name her face softened. "Aye," she said more gently. "He's allus seen me right. Even when she was on at me an' said she'd throw me out."

"Miss Bradshaw? Throw you out?" said Blake Hartley, surprised.

"She said she were going to throw me an' Sammy Woodley out. She'd allus promised she'd keep us on. Said we could stay in these cottages as long as we wanted. Then she changed her mind. Kept us guessin'. She were allus doing that. She liked tormenting us."

She turned abruptly and took up the axe to begin splitting logs once more. The inspector noticed she was left-handed. He was impressed by the deft way she swung the axe. Like a man.

"You're pretty good with that axe, Lizzie," he remarked.

"Sammy Woodley showed me," she said without stopping. "He's cack-handed like me. It's summat tha has to learn. There's a knack, tha knows. He worked in t'forestry afore he came here."

"I didn't know that," said Hartley. "Where?"

"T'Boltby Estate ower in Wharfedale," she grunted, still swinging her axe.

Hartley asked casually if the gardener had been back to his cottage.

"Not that I know of," she said. She seemed eager to get him away from the fire and, picking up an armful of logs, said she'd go to the cottage and check it out.

When she'd dumped her logs, she took a key from the row hanging just inside her door. "I have spares for every place here," she said. "I can soon tell you if Sammy's been back." They crossed the drive to the gardener's cottage and she let them in. He glanced around and asked if she'd any idea where he might be.

"No," she replied. "He never said where he went nor when he'd be back. He were a loner. He might have gone on to t'moors. He were allus goin' up there. Played at soldiers. Never really grew up. Lived in his own world. Made himself hideouts and the like. Stayed out all night sometimes pretending he were a soldier on patrol."

Inspector Hartley wasn't prepared for what he saw when they entered Woodley's cottage. Army daggers and bayonets were hanging on the walls. In an old wardrobe hung a paratrooper's smock complete with 'wings' on one shoulder. Alongside it was camouflage netting and a khaki balaclava. Lizzie said he bought it all from the surplus army stores in town.

He had a well-thumbed collection of military magazines. Hartley picked one up. It was a manual on self-defence and survival.

Lizzie Goodwin peered over his shoulder. "I told thee he was mad about soldiering, didn't I? Crazy about owt to do wi' t' army he was. He allus wanted to join t'army, but couldn't on account of his gammy leg."

"Aye," said Hartley. "I remember his leg. What happened to make him so lame?"

"He were knocked about as a lad by his father summat cruel. He never forgave him," she replied. "He never mentions it now, but he's never forgiven him."

Blake Hartley nodded thoughtfully. Such childhood cruelty scarred folk for life - and others they came in contact with later. Many of the men he put behind bars had been abused as children. He never forgave what crimes they'd done but he could always see how they came to do them.

There were three small rooms in Woodley's cottage: a kitchen scullery, a living room and a bedroom. The living room had a military flag across one wall and the bedroom was plastered with posters and pin-ups of soldiers and weapons. When he'd glanced around, Hartley asked if there were any guns. The housekeeper said she'd never seen any. Miss Bradshaw wouldn't have allowed it. But he did have a cross-bow, which he fired up on the moors.

Lizzie followed the inspector, watching him closely. Meeting her on her own ground loosened her tongue and she chatted away as he poked around. A tobacco pouch lay near Woodley's chair. Hartley picked it up. It didn't look like tobacco inside and when he smelled the contents, the sickly sweet smell of cannabis met him. Woodley was hooked on the stuff. Perhaps something harder if what he'd found in the vase was what he thought.

He replaced the pouch and said he'd better be going. She looked relieved and watched him go all the way up the drive. As soon as Hartley was out of sight she returned to her fire and began stoking it again, bringing out some clothing to burn with the rest of the stuff.

# CHAPTER TEN

"I didn't know yer were a vicar," mumbled Eli Cudworth through a mass of bandages. He was staring hard at Blake Hartley's clerical collar. "It's not one of yer disguises, is it? How can a copper be a vicar?"

And the Revd Detective Inspector Hartley pondered that question.

He'd been on his weekly visit to Riverdale Hospital, just outside Keighworth, and quite by chance had stumbled across Eli Cudworth in a side-ward. His arm was in splints and his head heavily bandaged. There were visitors at every bed he passed, but Eli was alone. The ward sister had asked him to call in.

The old man explained he'd been moved from Skiproyd Hospital for more surgery. He described how he'd been beaten up and the inspector listened in grim silence. "I'm sorry, Eli," he said gently when the old man had done. "Someone must have warned Woodley. He never showed up at The Bull."

"I know he bloody didn't!" exclaimed Eli. "That's why I'm in here!"

He went on to tell Hartley that he'd been tailed immediately he and his sergeant left Skiproyd and the Quereshis knew when they were coming back. He'd heard the Quereshis in contact with someone on their mobile phone. And the old man went on the tell the inspector more. He'd nothing to lose now.

Though he hadn't realised it, Eli was unwittingly running drugs. He'd picked up the vases for months from Woodley then taken them to an address in Manchester, where he worked another market. He thought the vases were imitations - good ones. Good enough to fetch a good price in the trade. He'd been paid well for moving them, but clearly had no idea what was in them. In Manchester the vases had been bought always by the same drug-trafficker.

Blake felt sorry for poor Cudworth and asked him if there was anything he could do. Anyone he could contact. "I've a daughter," he said. "She comes to visit me when she can. Lives at Kendal. Married a good feller so I've kept out of their way. I haven't been in touch since this happened an' she'll be worried sick. Could yer tell her where I am, boss?"

"Of course," said the inspector and jotted down the telephone number the old man gave him.

"You won't say owt about them vases, boss? I've tried to go straight for t'last twenty years. I don't want her to think I've gone off the rails again. Got to think about her kids, my grandsons. I don't want to queer their pitch going inside again."

Hartley smiled quietly and patted Eli's good arm. "No need to worry about that, Eli. You've done nowt wrong. I'll give your lass a ring and let her know where you are. And I'll see you when I come round again. Best get some rest now."

He patted the old man's shoulder again and left. But as he turned into the main ward, he almost collided with a huge bunch of flowers coming the other way. Hidden behind it was Superintendent Donaldson with his wife, Daphne.

Blake stood back to let the flowers pass. Then saw who they were and smiling broadly wished them good evening.

"Good evening, Hartley," barked his boss. His wife gave a stiff smile and nodded. Donaldson glanced at the inspector's collar. "Still on duty eh? Good for you." The inspector was about to say he was on his weekly visit, but Donaldson cut in with, "We're visiting Brigadier Braithwaite, Chairman of the Bench. Did you know he was in hospital? You ought to pop in and see him. Good for our public image when folk know we have a padre at the station, eh?"

Hartley asked which ward the brigadier was on. He didn't really want to go, as he'd more visits to make, but there was no way out.

"He's private," said Donaldson.

"Anything serious?" asked the inspector.

The Super lowered his voice and took a step nearer. He glanced at his wife who was looking the other way, then pointed to his crutch and whispered, "Prostate.."

"Catches up with us all in time - like death," Hartley replied pursing his lips.

Donaldson coughed awkwardly and threw his wife a quick glance. Daphne was fidgeting and looking at her watch, so he said they'd better be off. He remarked casually that he wanted to see Blake again the next day as soon as he got in. His wife gave her stiff smile and nod, then they swept along the corridor behind their bunch of flowers.

But the next day Donaldson was a different man, far from pleasant. He'd been reading Blake Hartley's report on the Bradshaw case and he wasn't at all happy with the way his inspector had tried to implicate Peter Fawcett. Donaldson would have none of it. Fawcett was clean, he said. Hartley had no concrete evidence, no 'factual data', a term he'd lifted from some criminal psychology book he'd been reading.

"You don't build up a case on non-factual data, Hartley," he lectured. "Hard facts are what I want. Not circumstantial guesses. We'll be laughed out of court if we don't produce factual data. You know what these lawyers are like." He seized on the murder weapon mentioned by Dr Dunwell. "Now if you find that, Hartley, you're halfway to solving the crime. You've nothing more factual than a murder weapon. More tangible than motives." He liked the sound of that so he said it again. "Yes, far more tangible than mere motives." Then he went on and on about factual data.

Blake was livid by the time he reached his office. Even more determined to go his own way and sod the Super! "The man's an idiot!" he growled, as he walked in.

"I wish I'd a fiver for every time you've said that, sir," said Sgt Khan, looking up from behind his desk. "I'd be able to retire."

"Don't joke about it, Khan," he said irritably. "The way things are going both of us might be on the retirement list soon. And you first!" He poured himself a cup of tea saying grimly, "Us two'll have to go it alone, Khan. Our Arthur's on Fawcett's side and he holds all the aces right now. We've still got to have ours dealt."

The inspector pondered his tea, speaking more to himself than to his sergeant. "Now let's go over all the events, Khan, one by one. Fawcett said he was at home when his aunt died. Yet when Lizzie rang he doesn't answer the phone. But his fancy woman does, saying he's busy. Then that chap Roe hears someone with a posh accent briefing Woodley to do a drop the same night. It could only have been Fawcett, couldn't it?"

"Wishful thinking, sir," said Khan. "Non-factual data!"

"Oh, don't you start!" said the inspector.

His sergeant smiled broadly. "But you may be right, sir. Have you considered that car he drives? It's pretty powerful. In that he'd be back at Grasby from The Grange in no time, and if he had a car-phone he'd be in touch with the lady you call his fancy woman, sir."

Inspector Hartley put down his cup. "I never thought of that, Khan. He could easily have told Jay Hussein to stall us and make it appear he was miles away from The Grange when the murder took place."

He rubbed his chin and they went over in detail what they'd gleaned: what Hartley had picked up from Wilf Roe; what Khan had picked up in Bradford; what Eli Cudworth had said in hospital. But still they couldn't pin anything concrete on Fawcett. No wonder he'd laughed at them as they left his home.

The break came after the choir practice at Ingerworth Church the following week. The older members adjourned to The Railway Tavern after practice night, meeting in the back parlour. Among them was Jack Clapham, Miss Bradshaw's family lawyer. When they'd ordered their drinks he said he wanted to speak privately with the inspector. He'd something to tell him about Miss Bradshaw. So they took their pints to a quiet part of the pub.

"The more I've been thinking about it," he began, "the more I felt you should know, Blake. I had a phone call from Miss Bradshaw the day before she died. It might have something to do with her death."

Blake wondered why it had taken so long for Jack Clapham to speak up …but then lawyers were like that. Canny as they come and taking their time before they say anything; so Blake said nothing but listened.

"She was very upset," Jack continued. "Said there was something fishy going on at The Grange. But when I asked her what, she said she couldn't tell me over the phone but would tell me when we met. What she wanted to do was change her will. She took me by surprise. I said I couldn't get over for a couple of days and she seemed happy with that."

"Any idea why she wanted to change it?" asked Hartley.

The other shrugged his shoulders, "None. She was very set in her ways. But she did tell me she was going to cut her nephew out of it and I thought that very strange."

Inspector Hartley raised his eyebrows. "She thought the sun shone out of him," he commented. "I wonder what he'd done to upset the old woman."

"You knew him from old, didn't you, Blake?" said Clapham. "When your mother worked at his place. Why on earth should she want to cut him adrift now? He's her only relative."

"Dunno," he said. "Wish I did. It'd shed a whole deal of light on the case. What exactly did you say to her, Jack?"

"I advised her not to act too hastily, like I do all our clients when they suddenly want to change wills. Old folk are like kids sometimes, especially when they're upset. They change their minds at whim. I told her to think it over. But she was adamant. She wanted to make a new will leaving out all the previous beneficiaries. Give everything to her favourite animal charity."

"Summat must have upset her badly," observed Blake.

"You know the rest, Blake. She died before I could meet her," said the lawyer.

"And so her old will stands?"

"Yes. It must."

"With her nephew as chief beneficiary doubtless?" asked Hartley.

"Of course. The housekeeper and gardener were the others. She left them the lodges where they live and a small annuity," said the lawyer. Then after a pause, "You must understand, Blake, this is strictly between ourselves. If ever her nephew found out…"

He left his sentence unfinished and looked hard at the inspector.

"Of course, of course, Jack," said Blake Hartley quickly. "My lips are sealed. I'm a priest - your priest." Then he murmured to himself looking into his drink, "You have switched the will for the deed, Fawcett, but your day of reckoning draws nigh."

"Pardon?" said the lawyer.

"Oh, nothing," said Blake Hartley. "Just a quotation which came to mind. You know what I'm like. It somehow seemed apt."

They turned the conversation to church business and joined the rest of the choir. When they left the pub, the inspector strolled home through the church graveyard, turning over what he'd just learned. He began humming softly to himself, then started singing a psalm softly as was his habit when he was happy. He'd got a vital lead on the Bradshaw case. He felt very satisfied with himself, but stopped singing as he passed the church. There he paused a while before hurrying on. Another, more sombre thought surfaced. Did his satisfaction stem from vengeance?

# CHAPTER ELEVEN

The forensic report on the powder Hartley had found in the vase had been submitted. It confirmed what the inspector had suspected. It was heroin. There were minute traces of plastic, too, probably from the container the drug had been in.

"We're right!" he said triumphantly, waving the report at his sergeant. "Somebody's been using those vases for drug-pushing. And there's no prize for guessing who. And I'd like to bet that the vase I took the samples from has already gone. Fawcett was on tenterhooks. He never took his eyes off it all the time I was there." But Inspector Hartley was wrong. When he and Khan went to The Grange next day, there were *two* vases on the mantelpiece. Moreover, the whole room had been cleaned up.

When they tried unscrewing the bases, they had great difficulty. They weren't the same as those Hartley had first seen. Those had been copies. The ones they saw now were the originals and their bases hadn't been touched in years. They'd been switched.

A movement in the mirror caught Hartley's eye as he replaced a vase. He turned quickly. There was no one there. But someone had been watching them. They heard movement in the hallway and hurried to the door, catching up with Lizzie Goodwin about to leave.

"Lizzie!" called out the inspector. "Come here!" She turned.

He expected to see her frightened. Alarmed at least. But she smiled. It was he who registered surprise. "Aye?" she said slowly. "What does tha want? I didn't expect to see thee here."

She lied. And she knew that he knew it.

"Why were you watching us just now? Why didn't you come in?"

She put on her simple stare. "I were just checking," she said. "Nowt wrong wi' that, is there? I wondered who it were. Tha could ha' been thieves." Hartley was thrown by her ready reply and she enjoyed his discomfort.

"Lizzie," he said, "who put those vases on the mantelpiece? There was only one when I called yesterday."

"I did," she replied brazenly. "I were cleaning t'other yesterday. T'whole place needed cleaning, but I had to wait till your lot had finished."

"You saw Mr Fawcett when he came?"

"Aye. He's me boss now. An' he's said me an' Sammy can stay on."

Hartley was getting nowhere. Somewhere along the line she was in cahoots with Fawcett and Woodley. Whatever had caused Elizabeth Bradshaw to cut her nephew from her will was the same reason she'd cut out her housekeeper and gardener.

The inspector rubbed his chin thoughtfully as she stared at him with a triumphant smile. He looked up suddenly and changed tack. "Tell me, Lizzie, who's going to win the Grand National next week? You were always good at picking winners." he said.

His question threw her a moment, but her face registered interest at once. She was a lifelong punter and as a boy Hartley had often seen her place bets.

"I'm putting my brass on Peter Piper," she said. He's earned me a bob or two already this season. Mr Fawcett is part owner, tha knows. He's keen on horses like me," she said proudly.

Hartley asked if she still used her old bookie, Jackman. She said yes.

"Then put a quid on Peter Piper for me, Lizzie," he said, slipping her a coin. "If I win we'll go evens, eh?"

She seemed pleased and pocketed his money before leaving. A very bemused Khan asked what it was all about.

"Another hunch, Khan," he said. "Another bit of non-factual data. If my hunch is right, she's been betting heavily recently."

"What makes you think that, sir?" asked Khan.

"A burnt wallet. It holds money even less easily than a burnt pocket. Come on. Let's get round to Harold Jackman's before Lizzie and see if my hunch is right."

They drove straight to Jackman's betting shop in town. The bookie and Blake Hartley were old friends from schooldays. Both found Keighworth a good place to work in. There was the usual bunch of punters glued to the telly, watching the racing, hardly looking round as the inspector and his sergeant entered. Hartley asked the clerk at the counter if he could see his boss and was shown into the office. Harold Jackman was totting up a ledger and glanced up as they went in. Then he closed his book and came forward to greet them. He'd often helped Hartley in the past when money had been laundered through his betting shop.

"I've come about one of your clients, Harold," he began. "Lizzie Goodwin."

"I've been half-expecting you," the other replied. "She's been laying heavy bets of late and I've been worried where she's been getting her brass." The bookie turned to his ledger and ran his finger down a column. "She lost a packet last week. Over a hundred quid. Not her scene at all. Yet she's cleared her account. Came in last night with these."

He turned and opened a safe behind him, pulling out a box full of notes ready for banking. On top was a bundle heavily stained with blood. Sgt. Kahn grimaced.

"She said she'd cut her finger badly," said Jackman.

"Looks more like she'd cut her throat!" Hartley exclaimed. "I'll have to take these, Harold, to let forensic have a dekko. Have you got a bag?"

The bookie produced a plastic bag and Hartley stowed the bundle safely in his pocket. As he wrote out a receipt he asked, "By the way, Harold, got a hot tip for the National?"

"Aye, Peter Piper. Want to place a bet?"

"I already have. Lizzie Goodwin's on her way with it."

The bookie laughed and locked his safe as the inspector went out, but Ibrahim Khan hung back a moment. "Here," he said quietly, slipping the bookie a quid. "Put this on Peter Piper, will you? I can't let my boss win all the time when he's been given such good tips! But keep quiet about it."

# CHAPTER TWELVE

Later that week, the Khans went to an antiques fair in Leeds. They were looking for a set of nineteenth century dining-chairs. Semina wanted furniture in keeping with their old house.

They spent some time mooching round the different stands, but didn't find what they wanted until they reached a display specialising in exactly what they were looking for. A Webb gate-legged table caught Semina Khan's eye. She thought the shop displaying it might have chairs to match. She looked at the name over the stand, "Elmet Antiques" and went in to find an assistant, while Khan wandered idly round the display.

He'd picked up a glass pomade jar shaped like a bear and was admiring it, when a voice behind him said softly, "Cute, isn't it?" He turned. Facing him with her alluring smile was Jay Hussein.

"So, Sergeant Khan, we meet again," she said sexily. "Looking for anything special? I've plenty on view."

"You can say that again," thought Khan, giving her the once-over. She was dressed in an even lower-cut top than that she'd worn at Grasby Manor. She'd a cleavage you could have posted a parcel in, and his attention switched from past antiques to present exhibits.

Realising she was playing with him, his eyes moved from her body to her face. "Yes, your display is very attractive," he said, playing her at her own game. "But tell me, what was this jar used for?" he added, holding up the jar.

"Hair cream. It's American. Used by men who fancied their chances," she smiled. "Do you fancy yours enough to buy it?"

He asked its price. It cost two hundred pounds and he replaced the jar quickly.

"I was simply curious that's all," he said. "Its shape attracted me." And felt like adding that that wasn't the only comely shape there which attracted him.

Another customer wanted attention and Jay Hussein excused herself. Semina Khan came over double-quick and asked her husband who the woman was he'd been talking to. It was obvious he knew her - knew her well!

"That, my dear, is Jay Hussein," he said. "The lady from Grasby Manor. The woman in the mirror at the Golden Pheasant. And now very much in the flesh here. She's the Karachi connection."

"She's certainly well connected!" said Semina, glancing across. "And so were you. Your lusty little eyes were wandering all over her."

Khan smiled. "A male privilege," he countered. Then he became serious. "Look, darling," he said, "she'll be back in a moment. You know nothing about her, understand? We've simply come to buy chairs. That's all. But when you meet her, find out all you can about this shop she works for, Elmet Antiques."

When she returned, the two women sized each other up. Jay Hussein spoke easily enough all the time. Nothing seemed to throw her. In that she was like Fawcett. Cool and polished – ruthless when she wanted to be.

She invited Semina to look over some chairs on display and as they moved away, Sergeant Khan picked up a leaflet. It seemed Elmet Antiques had shops all over the North. The headquarters were in Leeds.

"Quite a spread," he thought. "The perfect front for drug-pushing."

His wife returned. She'd been given the shop's address. It was only five minutes away. There was more on display there and it wouldn't take long to reach. Khan was footsore and edgy. He hated shopping and he'd had enough, but he said he'd go.

They'd barely got inside when Fawcett himself appeared from behind a curtained door. His office was the other side, along with the surveillance monitors. Cameras were everywhere and he'd seen them enter. At some unseen signal, the assistants melted away. Fawcett alone greeted them.

"Well, well, well! Sergeant Khan! What a pleasant surprise," he said silkily, shooting his cuffs as he approached. "And this beautiful lady, I assume, is the dear wife you told me about. The antiques connoisseur. How delighted I am to meet you, Mrs Khan."

He oozed charm, bowing low over Semina's hand and kissing it with old-fashioned gallantry.

"Jay tells me you're interested in Webb chairs to match a table," he said. "Let me know exactly what you want, Mrs Khan, and I'll find it. We've a large selection to choose from."

Semina didn't have to act her part. She loved antiques and took her time looking round. But another scenario was being played out between her husband and Fawcett. His patter was well rehearsed. He never stopped quipping and joking the whole time, flattering Semina non-stop while at the same time weighing up her husband.

He wasn't at all put out apparently by the sergeant turning up so unexpectedly. On the contrary he seemed to relish it. And though he lavished attention on his wife, he barely spoke to Khan. When he did, his eyes mocked him constantly. He was playing with Khan and beating him hands down and he knew that Khan knew he knew it.

He led them to some chairs beautifully turned in oak. "Here are some fine hardwood chairs set with waved top-rails that would match your table," he said.

"How much?" asked Semina.

"Around three thousand pounds," he said coolly.

"The set?" asked Sergeant Khan.

"No. Each," smiled Fawcett, and his eyes mocked Khan more than ever.

Khan gulped and eased his tie, asking if they had anything else. Fawcett smiled again; this time patronisingly. "As a matter of fact we have," he replied airily, and steered the couple across the room." "Not quite up to Webb's standard, but sufficient," he said. "In some ways I find them more attractive. Webb can be rather austere at times."

Fawcett, the epicure, had no time for austerity.

When Khan read the price tags he remarked he was more taken with them than the last lot. He said they'd go well with the table at home.

"If you really think so…" said Semina undecided.

"I do. No doubt at all" said Khan before she could change her mind. "I like them!"

She clinched the sale and began writing a cheque.

"We deliver next week," said Fawcett. "If they'd been less bulky I'd have delivered at once. But my little two-seater doesn't take much apart from myself - and whoever's joy-riding with me."

He gave his soft laugh then began to escort them to the door. They had to pass some vases on the way out. He paused by them, deliberately bringing Khan's attention to them. Among them was a pair of bronze vases identical to those at The Grange. He picked one up, his mocking eyes never leaving Khan's face. "I'd like you and Inspector Hartley to have these," he said. "One each. Inspector Hartley was rather taken by a similar pair at my aunt's. Alas, these are simply cheap reproductions. I give them away as freebies. Good for business, you know." He smiled again broadly, chuckling to himself as he passed one to Semina.

"Really, Mr Fawcett, you're too kind," said Semina. She examined the vase and asked what it was used for. It was clearly not simply for decoration.

"Funeral urns. Strange, isn't it, how fine art is often inspired by death?" he said quietly, more to himself than them.

"But far more inspired by life," said Khan.

Fawcett ignored him and began unscrewing the base, showing the inside to the sergeant. "The ashes were placed in here," he smirked. "The rest of the vase was used as a coffer for the family fortune.

Guarded by the spirits of the dead whose ashes lay beneath. That was the general idea. Funereal piggy-banks." He laughed as he screwed back the base. "But they can be used for a whole host of purposes," he added, handing it to Khan.

Khan found himself thanking the man, but he felt like throttling him. Then Fawcett passed him the second vase before ushering him from the shop, a vase under each arm and feeling foolish.

As they left, Jay Hussein entered and stood smiling alongside her boss at the door. As they passed the window outside, she waved cheerily at Khan, just as she'd done at Grasby Manor.

Semina waved back, but Khan stared stonily ahead and pushed his way through the Saturday crowds back to their car. They spoke little, but when his wife remarked what a charming man Fawcett was, he gave her a vase to carry.

# CHAPTER THIRTEEN

The following Monday, Blake Hartley visited his good friend Dr Augustus Dunwell, chief pathologist in the forensic team. Their friendship had grown ever since Dunwell had come to Keighworth some years before. They soon discovered they shared similar interests.

Blake Hartley was fascinated by all things medical. He'd dearly wanted to study medicine when leaving school but had not been able to. He'd had to leave at sixteen to train as a lab assistant. He'd joined the force after National Service in the Intelligence Corps. Hartley had a fine singing and speaking voice. So had Dunwell. They were both in the Keighworth Vocal Union and acted at times in Keighworth Little Theatre. And they shared similar tastes in whisky. And though Dunwell was a freemason like Superintendent Arthur Donaldson, he disliked him. So did Hartley.

Yet there was one marked difference. Where Hartley was a firm believer, Dunwell was an agnostic. He was ten years or so younger than the inspector. More rounded in the gut area. yet better dressed to the point of being dapper in a weighty sort of way. He was short-sighted and wore jam-jar bottom specs with thick black frames. He'd a habit of taking them off when he was thinking and breathing heavily on the lenses before cleaning them with his hankie. One suspected he'd done this from boyhood. Certainly he looked very boyish when he did it. He was almost bald on top, with one solitary lock of hair which he stroked carefully downwards, as if it somehow hid his baldness. It looked lost on the top of his head and flopped about when caught by the wind.

A confirmed bachelor, Gus Dunwell dined frequently with the Hartleys. He enjoyed their company and Mary's cooking. No mean cook himself, he was a gourmet and knew the best eating-houses for miles around. North country food he liked best of all. It was solid and filling and the good doctor had much to fill. But he had an off-putting tendency to discuss autopsies at meal-times. A tendency which had brought Ibrahim Khan to the brink of throwing up several times.

The pathologist turned in his chair as Hartley entered. "Ah, my favourite God-botherer," he said, rising and shaking the inspector's hand. "How's things in your neck of the woods?"

"If you're referring to the Bradshaw case, not very well. We haven't cracked it yet. Nowhere near. How's yourself, my little pagan?" Hartley replied.

"All the better for seeing you, Blake," the doctor beamed. Then his face changed and he looked grim. "I'm glad you called. Badly needed someone like you to talk to."

The inspector could see the pathologist was upset, which was unusual for him. He was a very phlegmatic character and it took a lot to upset him.

"What's up?" he asked.

Dr Dunwell bit his lip. "I've something...someone to show you. I meant to ring you once I'd finished my autopsy. Rotten business."

He took the inspector to the mortuary and said nothing till they arrived. There was a corpse on the autopsy bench. He pulled back the sheet covering it.

"They brought this kid in yesterday. He's from your patch, Blake. Know him?"

Inspector Hartley looked at the young wasted face. He knew the lad all right.

"Aye," he said slowly, pain creeping into his eyes as the pathologist replaced the sheet. "He was called Banjo, but his real name's Brooks. Paul Brooks. A bit of a tearaway, but I'd always a soft spot for him. He'd have made out with a bit of luck. What's happened?"

"Suicide," said Dunwell.

"Suicide," echoed, the inspector. "At his age! He's barely fifteen. What made him do it?"

"Drugs. He's been on ecstasy. Full of the stuff. And not very good quality stuff at that," said Dr Dunwell.

"I knew he was on drugs. His mum told us. But why suicide?" asked Hartley.

"After the first high it produces depression. Those hooked on it go into a downward spiral if they can't get enough. His mother found him hanging in his bedroom last night. And she found these as well." He handed the inspector a couple of tablets in a plastic bottle.

"What is it?"

"Crack. It's suddenly being distributed in Keighworth. The drugs intelligence officer has no idea who's pushing it. He's had his plants on the look-out for weeks, but no-go. The worst part is it's being flogged to kids like Banjo. Even younger. And he's been taking some pretty stiff cocktails, I can tell you. You should see what I found inside him."

They left the lab and went back to his office. He had the forensic report on Miss Bradshaw's wallet and the blood on the handkerchief and banknotes. In both cases it matched the dead woman's. Whoever had handled the wallet had lifted the banknotes from it.

"D'you think that's why the old girl was bumped off?" asked Dunwell.

"Could be," said Hartley. "Yet it seems odd they left her wallet. If they'd knocked her off for her money, they'd have taken the wallet and dumped it somewhere else. Not left it next to the body. And how come Lizzie was burning it?"

"D'you think she killed her?" said Dunwell.

"She's certainly on the list," replied the inspector. "On the other hand, she could have lifted the wallet when she found Miss Bradshaw dead. I'm giving her the benefit of the doubt and letting Lizzie be for the time being. She's a lot more to tell, but if I lean on her she'll clam up tight."

Hartley read through the report, then asked if Miss Bradshaw had died instantly.

"More than likely," said the pathologist. "Probably before she hit the deck. That first blow was so powerful, it penetrated her skull. The other blow was struck as she lay on the floor. Severed her carotid. Must have been a messy business. Whoever did it would have been covered with blood."

"So the murderer's shoes would have blood on them?"

"Yes. They'd have been paddling in it," said Dunwell. "I'm surprised we didn't find more traces. Whoever killed Miss Bradshaw made damned sure their tracks were covered. The carpet had been thoroughly cleaned before they left."

"Lizzie was burning some slippers on the fire where I found the wallet," said the inspector.

"If I were you, I should get forensic down there double quick to sift through it," said Dunwell. "Before she starts messing about with what's left. By the way, Blake, any sign of the weapon?"

"Not a sausage. All we found was an old rusted axe in the woodshed. It hadn't been used for weeks. Anyhow, its blade was too thick. Nowt like the one you said killed her."

"No meat-cleavers about the place? They'd fit the bill," suggested Dunwell.

The inspector shook his head and the doctor began chattering about food. It was never far from his mind. But Hartley only half-listened. His mind was racing and in his mind's eye, he went over the contents of the room where Elizabeth Bradshaw had died. The old fireplace had been blocked off and gas installed. No fire-irons or anything there. Nothing remotely like the murder weapon.

He turned to the walls. A family oil-painting over the fireplace. The Georgian mirror he'd glimpsed Lizzie Goodwin in. Some water colours by a local artist. And on the opposite wall the Cromwellian armour and crossed battle-axes. He paused. Yes, the battle-axes!

"Idiot!" he said to himself. "By George! Why didn't I think of it before?

Dr Dunwell stopped in mid-sentence. "What the devil are you on about, Blake?" he said completely foxed. "You haven't been listening to me, have you? Day-dreaming as usual. I could tell by the look on your face you were miles away."

"Dreams are more vivid than facts," said the inspector, smiling. "The murder weapon. I think I may have found it, Gus. Hanging on Miss Bradshaw's wall. The battle-axes there would fit the bill exactly."

The pathologist's face lit up. "They'd also fit the pattern of murder," he exclaimed. "Whoever killed the old lady could easily have replaced the weapon on the wall once he'd cleaned it up. That way, he'd no need to hide it. Clever. Very clever! We're up against a real Moriarty here, Blake."

"So it can't be Lizzie," mused Hartley.

"Lizzie Goodwin? Good God, no! She's only ninepence to the shilling. This killer's a genius. He's done exactly the sort of thing I'd do if I were going to bump off someone I didn't like. Donaldson, for example. I'd cover my tracks, then feed my ego by challenging you lot and leaving the murder weapon in full view. It's classic. Psychopaths are so self-centred they just have to show off. All the ones I've met keep cuttings of their crimes to boast about. The tabloids are the spin-doctors of criminals. They trumpet their foul deeds far and wide. Believe me, Blake, your killer's a Moriarty."

"You make it all sound so very elementary, my dear Dunwell," smiled Blake Hartley. "Almost too elementary to be believed."

# CHAPTER FOURTEEN

Sammy Woodley had been recognised in Adderton. He'd visited the pub briefly, then disappeared before the police could arrive. The pub's set of darts went with him, and Inspector Hartley was puzzled. He thought Woodley was in one of Fawcett's safe houses, lying low till they could get him clear. Woodley's appearance in Adderton made the inspector think again. He wasn't hiding up with Fawcett, and that was strange. The last thing Fawcett would have wanted was Woodley being picked up. He'd have sung loud and long and blown the whistle on him. He thought Fawcett would have had Woodley where he could keep his eyes on him.

Hartley was in for yet another surprise. Abdul Quereshi's brother Saddique turned up - very dead in the river, some miles downstream from Adderton, near Ilkesworth, two days after a warrant had been put out for his arrest. The drugs squad in Bradford had enough to nail the whole gang. Sergeant Khan discovered that when he was sent to Bradford by Donaldson to make his peace. The black pusher called Crack was in fact Detective Sergeant Peter Horrocks, who'd been working undercover for months at The Old Ram till they'd enough evidence to pull in the Quereshis. Khan's sudden appearance had almost messed up the whole operation!

When the warrant went out for their arrest, the brothers and most of their gang went to ground. The murky waters of the River Wharfe sent ripples all the way to Bradford when the elder Quereshi's body was found floating in it

As soon as they were informed, Hartley and Khan went straight to Ilkesworth. They found Qureshi's body sprawled on the riverbank, near where he'd been fished out. Hartley pulled back the sheet they'd thrown over him. There were deep wounds round his neck. He'd been garrotted before he'd been chucked in the river.

"What d'you make of those, Khan?" he asked. The windpipe had been cut through, so tight had been the garrotte. The corpse gaped back at the sergeant, revealing a goldmine of capped teeth. Terror still held his staring eyes.

Khan flicked a quick glance and looked away. He'd already begun to pale and looked studiously at the clouds above. He didn't reply to the inspector's question.

"I'd say those two punctures under his left ear were caused by darts," said Hartley, to himself.

Khan risked another quick glance.

"Would darts have penetrated so deeply, sir?" he asked.

"Not normally. But if they'd been fired from a weapon - a cross-bow – well, that's a very different kettle of fish. But this," he said, pointing to the vicious weal, "has been done by piano wire."

He turned the dead man's hands over. There were deep cuts across the palms. "Look, Khan. See these?" said the inspector. "He tried to struggle clear and the wire cut his hands. With a guy this size, whoever bumped him off must have been very strong."

Khan didn't look. He took his inspector's word for it and asked if he thought Woodley had done it. It certainly tied in with what they knew about him.

"More than likely," replied Hartley. "But why should he want to kill Quereshi? He was part of their set-up." Then he stood up and mused, "Unless Quereshi had been sent to do a hit job on *him*!"

Dr Dunwell arrived not long after, striding across the field towards them bellowing, "Don't touch anything! I don't want heavy-handed coppers messing things up before I've had a proper look. You haven't moved him, have you, Blake?" Then he knelt by the body and began his examination.

"Don't panic," said the inspector. "He hasn't moved an inch. He's been waiting for you to come. Said he was getting quite chilly."

The pathologist ignored him, concentrating on his job. Hartley asked how long Quereshi had been dead.

"Difficult to say, old fellow," he replied. "At a guess I'd say around twenty-four hours. He's been in the water at least that long. Yet the rats haven't got at him. They usually wait a day or two before they have a nibble. I'll know better when I've opened him up and have a good poke around his lungs and gut."

Sergeant Khan moved out of earshot. He was growing paler by the minute.

The pathologist turned the dead man's neck and saw the two punctures. "Hello, who's been here? Dracula?"

"The count would have needed jaws like a shark to get that spread. They're made by darts," said Hartley, smugly.

"Look. Who's supposed to be the pathologist here? Me or you?" said Dunwell, glancing up. "But you could be right. And whoever did the dirty deed made doubly sure by damned near taking his head off garrotting him."

The doctor finished his initial examination and stood up. Khan looked relieved and came back.

"Talking about heads. That reminds me," he said, wiping his hands. "I must give Mary a new recipe for sheep's head broth and dumplings. Got it from the cook at the Nag's Head yesterday. Good solid stuff. He also served sheep's brains on toast. Delicious!"

There was an audible retch behind them. He turned. Khan was holding a handkerchief to his mouth.

"You all right, Khan?" he asked.

Khan shook his head and moved off back to the car.

Dunwell shrugged his shoulders and wiped his glasses before peering down at the dead man. "Big chap," he commented. "Whoever did him in must have been strong."

"As big as Quereshi?" asked the inspector.

"No. Smaller, but very powerful. He attacked from behind. See how that scar angles down to the back of the neck. The killer had to pull well down, so he must have been smaller. But he's strong. Oh, yes, he's strong. Dangerous."

He asked Inspector Hartley if he'd any idea who might have done it. Hartley said Sammy Woodley would fit the bill and Dunwell asked if they knew where he was.

"Could be anywhere from Keighworth to Kingdom Come," said Hartley.

Dunwell went nearer the river and stared upstream. The wind caught the solitary wayward lock of hair on his bald head. He pulled it back into place. "If I were you, Blake," he said at length, "I'd have a good look up there. Let's say Adderton or Boltby Forest. It'd take a day for a stiff to float down this far from there. The river's quite steady this time of year."

Blake Hartley recalled what Lizzie had said about Woodley going back to those woods to play out childhood fantasies. And he wondered. But all he said was "You could be right, Gus. We'll have a good look round up there." Then he added as they strolled back to their cars "You know, Gus, when I saw Quereshi lying there dead, I couldn't help thinking of young Banjo in your morgue. I felt some kind of justice had been done."

"More like dog eating dog," grunted the pathologist. "If you're going to bring divine intervention into it, then it's a pity God didn't act earlier."

Inspector Hartley remained silent.

"But I must confess, Blake," Gus Dunwell continued, "I sometimes wish I had your beliefs. I'd cheerfully send all drug-pushers to the hottest part of hell. And keep them there for ever."

Sgt Khan was standing by his car. The colour had come back to his face, but he was keen to get away and got into the car before Quereshi's body was brought to the adjacent ambulance. Hartley joined him and opened the window. Dunwell remembered something and came across to tell him.

He said forensic had confirmed that one of the axes on the wall was the murder weapon. They'd found Miss Bradshaw's blood between the blade and socket. But whoever had used the weapon had worked damned hard cleaning it, the carpet, too.

Inspector Hartley thanked him and drove off, but he was in for another surprise before the day was out. He'd just finished his tea when Lizzie Goodwin rang. She said Woodley had come back. She thought she'd seen him in his cottage and was terrified. She begged Inspector Hartley to come at once.

Hartley groaned. He didn't feel at all like turning out. She was probably imagining things, he told his wife. It had been a long day and all he wanted to do was settle back with a good book and whisky by his hearth before he turned in.

He glanced through his window as a storm threatened. It was early evening yet the sky was already black, the sun smothered by a mass of cloud rolling in over the Pennines. As he left home, the storm broke. The whole valley erupted in a spectacular flash of lightning which ripped the valley in two and thrilled him to the core. The drama on such nights had moved him from boyhood, and he mused as he drove through it. The chaos of the storm was like crime: wild vicious forces unleashed on an unsuspecting land; evil launched on an ordered world.

Lines from "King Lear" came to his mind as the rain lashed his windscreen and the lightning lit up the road ahead. One of Keighworth's down-and-outs, a bundle of sodden rags, staggered down the pavement into a derelict building for shelter, and the line: "Poor naked wretches wheresoe'er you are, That bide the pelting of this pitiless storm…" ran through his head.

And the inspector wondered where the half-wit Woodley was. Probably cowering in some hovel he'd made for himself on the moors.

Lizzie Goodwin stood waiting at the door of her cottage. The lights were blazing in Woodley's cottage opposite, but there was no sign of Woodley. An old woman accompanied Lizzie, her friend from the estate. Probably the only friend she had. She told the inspector she'd gone for her as soon as she'd spotted Woodley, but when they'd returned, he'd disappeared.

She didn't seem as scared as she'd made out over the phone. She was more frightened of the storm for it certainly loosened her tongue. "This storm on top o' seeing Sammy Woodley is enough to drive you stark staring mad!" she said as the inspector got out of his car.

"Aye. We was both scared silly," echoed the old biddy at her side.

She peered wide-eyed at the inspector from under a dripping brolly. She'd pulled her head-scarf tightly round her head and buttoned up a dirty raincoat to the top. She looked as if she'd walked straight out of a Hogarth painting. She was small, bandy-legged and grossly overweight. Standing side by side, she and Lizzie looked like a comedy act. It became one when they spoke.

"This is Sally Webster," said Lizzie, looking down at her friend. "She lives just over there on t'estate. We've been waiting for thee ever since I phoned, haven't we, Sally?"

"We have that," her friend replied on cue.

"We'd almost given thee up, hadn't we, Sally?"

"We had that," confirmed the other.

Inspector Hartley said he was sorry but he'd come as soon as he could. He'd sent a patrol car on ahead.

"I know," said Lizzie. "An' they've gone on looking for him. But he'll be away ower t'moors by now. They'll never find him once he gets up there. Anyway, tha'd best come in, inspector."

Blake followed her into the cottage, glad to get out of the pouring rain. He noticed at once a scented smell which he couldn't place at first. It wasn't perfume, and in any case Lizzie didn't use perfume It was something heavier.

When they got inside Lizzie seemed more at ease. Too much so, thought Hartley who asked her when she'd seen Woodley.

"Just before I rang thee," she said and she trotted out the details like a well rehearsed set-piece. "I ran straight to Sally's and rang from there, didn't I, Sally?"

Her friend nodded dutifully.

Lizzie widened her eyes and pointed dramatically outside. "I saw him limping down t'drive. I'd no lights on 'cos it were thundering an' I'm flayed o' storms. But it were him all right. I'd recognise him anywhere wi' that limp."

"So would I," said Sally, not to be left out.

"Did you actually see his face?" asked the inspector.

"Well not exactly. Not full on, so to speak. He had his coat-collar turned up and his cap down. But it were him all right," Lizzie said emphatically.

"I'll have a look round Woodley's place," said Hartley going to the door.

The patrol had been there before him. Once they'd checked Woodley wasn't there, they'd left to search the estate. Nothing had been moved. It was exactly as it had been the last time he'd been there.

The air was dank, foisty. The air of an unlived-in room. It was almost a fortnight since Woodley had disappeared. Yet there was something different since the inspector's last visit. The air in the cottage held the same fragrant smell he'd noticed at Lizzie Goodwin's. It was the unmistakable smell of Turkish cigarettes. And Hartley recalled where he'd smelled them before.

"Grasby Manor. And also when I met him here at The Grange" he thought to himself.

He'd seen enough and hurried back to Lizzie's. She was completely at ease and had even gone to the trouble of making him a cup of tea. She asked him if he'd found anything. She didn't look directly at him as she asked the question and he thought he detected a sly smile on her lips.

"No," he said. "But tell me, Lizzie. What sort of cigarettes did Sammy smoke? Expensive ones?"

She looked up in surprise.

"No. He rolled his own. Cheap stuff. An' he kept well out o' Miss Bradshaw's way when he did smoke. She were dead against smoking. Even Mr Fawcett didn't light up when she were about."

Inspector Hartley was puzzled. There was no sign at all of Woodley. Nothing had been moved in his cottage. Why should she say she'd seen him when she hadn't? Was Fawcett pulling another red herring across his path and using Lizzie to draw it?

He'd dearly have liked to question her about the wallet and money, but the time wasn't right. She'd clam up. Give her enough time and she'd tell all. And he knew she'd tell Fawcett about his asking about Woodley's cigarettes. That would give Fawcett something to think about. Make him realise he'd made a gaffe.

Before he left, the patrol car returned. They'd found nothing. Someone had said they'd seen a car parked in a lay-by near the moors, but when they'd got there it had gone.

"Woodley couldn't drive," said Hartley, "so it couldn't have been him."

Hartley had seen enough and drained his tea, wishing Lizzie and her friend goodnight before he made his way back home. The storm had blown over but it was dark; too dark for him to do anything else. He decided he'd pay a visit to that lay-by first thing and have a nose round when it was light. Then he drove home and had enough time to enjoy one whisky before he turned in.

The air was fresh the next morning. He stood on the edge of the moors drinking it in, letting his eyes rove across the purple expanse of heather before him. Bank on bank of it rose to a cloudless sky and he let the sunshine soak in.

On the skyline stood a row of shooting-butts. As a lad, for some years he'd acted as a beater in the grouse season, driving the birds towards those butts where the gentry waited. At first, he'd found it exciting. But as he grew into his teens, he began to loathe the whole business, just as he grew to hate all killing. It sickened him seeing beautiful birds blown out of the sky. One minute warm living creatures. The next, lifeless bundles of feathers dropping earthwards.

The very last time he'd been up there, he'd acted as gun-loader. He recalled the event as he stood by his car looking over the moor. He remembered how the young Peter Fawcett had revelled in the slaughter. How eager and elated his face had been as he snatched gun after gun from his keeper in an orgy of killing.

And he recollected how the older men had complimented Fawcett and how self-satisfied the boy had been. How, when he looked at the heap of dead birds, he'd given the same strange chuckle he still gave.

Then Blake Hartley was brought from his memories with a start. "Grand day, isn't it?" said a broad-spoken voice behind him. It was the farmer from the neighbouring farm. He'd been walking round checking his sheep. Hartley turned to greet him and began chatting.

He asked about the car in the lay-by. A red one, the patrol had said. The farmer said he'd seen a red one there often recently, a vintage two-seater. But every time he appeared on the scene, the car drove off quickly before he could see who was in it. "Reckon somebody was having it off with somebody else's wife," he said with a wink.

"Aye," laughed Hartley. "There's a lot of it going on these days. Too much bother for me. Too much covering up to do. And I dread to think what would happen if the wife found out!"

The farmer laughed and went on his way. When he'd gone, Inspector Hartley had a closer look at the sandy soil in the lay-by. There were marks of a broad-wheeled car, made by tyres of the kind Fawcett had on his Alvis.

But most interesting of all was the black stub of a cigarette he found in the heather at the side of the lay-by. A Turkish cigarette. Smiling to himself, he picked it up and put it carefully in the plastic bag he always carried. Then he drove off.

# CHAPTER FIFTEEN

The breaking of The Old Ram drugs ring sparked off wholescale panic among Bradford's pushers. Abdul Quereshi was the first to go to ground. Like a trapped rat, he moved from one hideout to another as the net closed round him. In the end he ran out of bolt-holes and in desperation fled to Grasby Manor to seek Fawcett's help.

The first Fawcett knew of his arrival was when he heard the racket the prowler dog was making outside. It had cornered an intruder inside the high perimeter. Someone had climbed in unannounced and the dog had him pinned against the wall. The hounds inside the house added their din, till Fawcett shut them up. Carter, the handyman, was working in the garage and took his time reaching the terrified intruder. He knew his dog would keep him safe till he got there

At the time, Fawcett was in his study, and couldn't see what was up. He went into his lounge, where he was joined by Jay Hussein. "We seem to have an uninvited guest," he said peering through the window, enjoying the spectacle as the terrified intruder tried to keep the hound back and began yelling for help.

Carter was also enjoying it and ambled over slowly, letting the dog snap and slaver as the cornered man tried frantically to keep it at bay with a battered suitcase he carried. He was dishevelled and unshaven, looking for all the world like a tramp. So much so, Fawcett didn't recognise him at first.

But when Carter saw who he was and began laughing and led him to the house, Fawcett exclaimed, "Good God! It's Abdul Quereshi! The bloody fool! Why the hell is he coming here? He'll lead the police straight to us." Anger mingled with alarm in his face. Gone was all the suavity and humour of a moment before. He rarely lost his cool, but he did now and it didn't go unnoticed by the woman at his side.

"You're going to take him in, aren't you, Peter?" she said, and there was pleading in her voice.

He cut her short with an impatient gesture and remained watching Quereshi approach the house. He said nothing till Carter rang the bell. "I hope to God he hasn't been seen coming here," Fawcett said at length, walking away from the window back into the room. He looked more angry than ever and glared into the fire. When the bell rang, he snapped "Answer it!"

Jay Hussein left the room and as soon as she'd gone, he went to the Sheraton near the door. He pressed a switch under the lip of the table and a drawer slid open. He took a pistol from it, checked the magazine, then put the gun in his pocket, before returning to the fireplace. By the time the others came in, he appeared as calm and nonchalant as ever.

But Quereshi's appearance surprised him. He was exhausted and broken. He'd lost weight and seemed to be shrinking into the heavy overcoat he wore. It was ripped down one side where he'd snagged it climbing a fence, and, like his trousers, it was caked in mud. Gone was all his old arrogance. He was a frightened fugitive. On the run and done in.

Fawcett ran his eye over him contemptuously, though he welcomed him courteously enough. "Abdul, old fellow, I thought you'd gone to foreign parts. I heard about the police busting your set-up and assumed you'd carried out the usual drill," he said smoothly, all the time keeping his hand on the gun in his pocket.

Quereshi was distraught. His brother's death on top of the police raid had unnerved him. He ran his hand through his hair. "The usual drill didn't work this time. You've got to help me, Mr Fawcett," he began.

"Got to?" said Fawcett. "I haven't got to do anything. You know the rules of the game as well as myself, Abdul. Every man for himself when the game is up."

"Get me away to Karachi, Mr Fawcett," pleaded the other. "I know you can. Please!"

Fawcett stopped smiling.

He asked how Quereshi had got to the Manor, if anybody had seen him. Quereshi said he'd slipped out of Bradford unrecognised as far as he knew. He'd caught the bus to Skiproyd then thumbed a lift to Gurton. He told the driver he was going to Kendal when he'd dropped him off at Gurton cross-roads. He'd hiked the rest of the way across the fields. He was quite sure nobody had seen him.

"Like hell!" thought Fawcett. "Folk round here have eyes in the backs of their heads." But he said nothing, only continuing to look disdainfully at the crumpled figure before him. Quereshi broke under his cold stare and turned to Jay Hussein, speaking to her rapidly in a border dialect between Pakistan and Afghanistan. They both came from the same tribe there.

Fawcett couldn't understand them and asked what they were discussing. He told them to keep to standard Urdu.

"Abdul's appealing to our blood-tie," she explained. She looked uneasy. "He wants me to help and he knows I can't refuse."

She stared at Fawcett with a hint of defiance. It registered and he turned to Quereshi. "We're all bound by blood in this game," he said. Then he let the others hang on his silence before he said, "Yes, you can stay, Quereshi. You'll be safe enough here if you do as I say till I can get you away."

The other two looked relieved. Quereshi said he'd pay well, pay him from the money he carried. Fawcett looked surprised and his attitude altered. He asked him how much he'd got. "Ten grand…for starters," said Quereshi. The surprise heightened.

"For starters?" echoed Fawcett, eyeing Quereshi's suitcase greedily. "So you've brought something more than your pyjamas and toothbrush in that case?"

He laughed lightly and for the first time Quereshi smiled. "If I get back to Karachi in one piece, you'll be a very rich man, Mr Fawcett. I give you my word. Jay here can vouch for that."

"The bank-code? You have the bank-code I know," said Fawcett immediately. And there was no mistaking the eagerness in his voice as he nodded at Jay Hussein. "You have the other half of her father's bank-code?"

"And I can use it only when I arrive safely in Karachi," said Quereshi cannily. He knew he held an ace now.

Fawcett asked how he'd come by the other half of the code. He'd always known Jay Hussein held part of it. To have the entire code was to have the key to a fortune. All Karachi knew that.

"My brother and I had this agreement," said Quereshi. "Jay's father gave him the other half of the code. My brother was to marry her, you know. It had all been arranged."

"No. I didn't know," said Fawcett, obviously surprised. "More blood-ties?" he added whimsically.

Jay Hussein glanced across at Quereshi "Of course," she said. "Our marriage has been arranged for some time." Fawcett didn't believe her but said nothing, letting Quereshi have his say.

"Saddique entrusted the code to me, in case..." he said, then paused and bit his lip. "In case, anything happened to him. Life is unpredictable."

"Very," said Fawcett, unmoved, and thought, "Who'd have thought he'd let a half-wit like Sammy Woodley jump him?" He turned and poured himself a drink, but watched the others closely through the mirror over the table. Then he returned. "How very fraternal of Saddique to leave you the code," he said. Then he turned to Jay. "And the bride-to-be? Does she keep her part of the contract as well as the code?"

She nodded, but couldn't hold his eye.

"I hope you'll honour old Hussein's trust, Abdul. Make sure Jay inherits once you've clinched the deal. None of this wifely goods and chattels nonsense."

"Honour means everything to us," he said.

"I should hope so, my dear boy," said Fawcett, smiling. "Your people are renowned for it. More than could be said for some."

He took a sip of his drink, expecting Quereshi to say more. But he remained silent.

"Do you have the code now?" he said suddenly.

It was Abdul's turn to smile. "Now that would be telling, wouldn't it? It's my passport to freedom and it's essential to always hang on to your passport, isn't it, Mr Fawcett? We both know that. Only if I reach Karachi safely do we all live happily ever after. Like I said. You'll be well paid for getting me out. I promise."

Fawcett bit his lip angrily. He didn't like being talked to like that. Quereshi was playing with him.

He took his hand off his gun and offered Quereshi one of his cigarettes, lighting it for him because the other's hand shook so. He asked if Quereshi wanted a drink. He said he'd have a long scotch and a sandwich. He was famished.

"Jay will fix something," said Fawcett. Then more pleasantly, "Sit down, old chap. You look done in."

Fawcett continued to observe him closely while Quereshi wolfed the plate of sandwiches Jay brought him. He asked what had happened since they'd last met. Quereshi told him. How they'd been set up and how the police had cleaned out The Old Ram. How Quereshi's sidekicks had all been arrested and he'd got away by the skin of his teeth.

"How much did your people know?" asked Fawcett.

"Nothing more than they needed to know," said Quereshi, gulping his drink.

"They know nothing about me? The set-up here?"

"Absolutely nothing. You have my word. You once said, we must never let our left hand know what our right hand is doing. Remember?" Quereshi replied.

Fawcett stared idly at him and drew on his cigarette. He was satisfied as much as he could be that Quereshi was telling the truth.

He wandered to the window.

"Good," he said softly. "Because if the police get wind of me, we're all done for. You most of all. Our set-up will collapse like a pack of cards, and we don't want that to happen, do we, old fellow?" He turned and said more grimly. "Your brother paid the price for being off-guard. I don't want to finish up like him. And Jay here has her dowry to think of, eh?"

He let the significance of his words sink in, then dropped his eyes to the suitcase Quereshi still clutched. "It's going to be dicey getting you away. It'll cost a bomb. How much did you say you have?"

Abdul opened the case. It was packed with notes. Fawcett's eyes glittered greedily. There was at least a hundred grand there. "Leave it with Jay," he ordered. "It'll pay for your keep and travelling expenses. We've quite a cosy bolt-hole here, built for emergencies some years ago. A bit cramped, but safe enough if anyone from the police comes poking around. The last time it was used was by a priest on the run...about four hundred years ago."

He gave a soft chuckle, but Quereshi didn't appreciate his remark.

"My worry now," continued Fawcett, "is another priest may pop up at any moment, a policeman-priest. And he won't be on the run. Quite the contrary. He'll be after us and he has Allah on his side"

That remark, too, was lost on the other, who finished off the last of his food. Fawcett pressed a button near the fireplace and Carter appeared.

"Take Mr Quereshi to the room over the stabling, Carter," he said. "If we have unexpected callers, get him to the priest-hole at once. And on no account is he to leave the premises. Understand?"

Carter nodded, then growled, "Aye, sir. T'dogs'll see to that."

When they'd gone, Fawcett examined the suitcase. He casually picked up a bundle of notes and let his eye rove over the rest, before tossing the bundle back into the case and closing it. He told Jay Hussein to put it in the wall-safe.

"I should count it before you put it away, my dear," he said. "And give our friend a receipt. We don't want him accusing us of stealing, do we?"

"You *are* going to help him, aren't you?" she asked anxiously.

"Of course, my dear girl. One way or another we're all going to help each other, eh? That's how it's always been. One good deed and all that. I gave him my word, didn't I? And I, too, am a man of honour."

He smiled and poured himself another drink, returning to the window. In the fields next to the garden a tractor chugged to and fro on the neighbouring farm. Old Fothergill was driving it. Fawcett watched him a moment, before murmuring to himself, "A penny to a pound, there's one blighter who'll have seen Quereshi come here."

He lifted his eyes to the horizon. In the distance stood Boltby Forest. "And there's a bigger problem," he thought. "Sammy Woodley."

# CHAPTER SIXTEEN

Lizzie Goodwin clammed up tightly when Blake Hartley confronted her with the burnt wallet and banknotes. He visited her again a couple of days after she claimed she'd seen Woodley. He asked her yet again to go over the events of that night.

What she said didn't tie up at all with her previous statement, but he let her ramble on, before he quite suddenly switched to the wallet. Then her face set and she went sullen. Tight-lipped and buttoned up.

When he started writing in his notebook, it seemed to unnerve her. She asked if he was any closer to finding out who'd done the murder. "Aye," he replied slowly. "We're getting closer, Lizzie. Very close. It's been difficult, but we're getting there. We'll find out who's done it. You can be sure of that, Lizzie." She scowled across at him, but her scowl disappeared when he took out a plastic bag containing Miss Bradshaw's blood-stained handkerchief. "I think you recognise this, Lizzie, don't you?" he said quietly.

"It's hers," she gasped.

"Then how did it come to be in the kitchen waste-bin?" asked Hartley. She shrugged her shoulders and wouldn't meet his eye. He waited patiently. "Did you put it there, Lizzie?" he said at length. "I want to know."

She took a deep breath and answered, "Aye." He asked her why she hadn't told him before.

"Tha never asked," she said insolently.

"And it's Miss Bradshaw's blood that's on it," he said. "You know that, don't you?" She coloured deeply and he said, "I think you'd better come clean, Lizzie. It's for your own good, you know."

She bit her lip, then it all came out in a rush.

"I took it to wipe her wallet on. I took it 'cos it were t'only way of getting me own back. She owed me a month's wages, the stingy bitch. An' when I saw her wallet lyin' there stuffed wi' money, well, it were like a godsend."

The inspector asked if she'd touched anything else lying there. She shuddered and shook her head. He waited for her to say more, but there was no more to come.

"Lizzie," he said gently, "you've put yourself in a right awkward spot. It might be said you killed her…"

"I didn't! Honest, I didn't!" she exclaimed, flushing deeply again and wringing her hands. "I might have hated her, but not enough to kill her. Tha must have some idea who did it, inspector, 'cos it weren't me."

Her voice was panic-stricken. Her eyes held the fear of a trapped animal. But Inspector Hartley said nothing. He put away his pen and notebook and strolled to the window, looking up at The Grange, as if he saw the answer to her question there. When he spoke, it was more to himself than Lizzie.

"Time will tell," he said quietly. "And time is running out fast for whoever killed Miss Bradshaw." Then he wished her good morning and left.

He'd barely left her cottage when she hurried to the phone. She dialled Fawcett and told him what Blake Hartley had said. She was almost incoherent and he tried to calm her. He wanted to know exactly what she'd told the inspector.

"It's a pity about the wallet," he said, when she'd done. "But, Lizzie, you're quite sure you didn't say anything about our arrangements? Nothing about the vases, eh?"

By now she was snivelling and spoke in a hurt voice. "Sir, you know me better than that. I've never let you down."

"My dear Lizzie, of course you haven't," he replied soothingly, but the relief in his voice was transparent. "You've always been an absolute brick…about everything…as long as we've known each other. And that's a very long time now, isn't it?"

There was a pause and she surprised him by suddenly bursting uncontrollably into tears. He'd never known her weep so and asked what was up.

"Sir, I'm so flummoxed," she wailed. "I can't think straight. I keep getting the bad headaches again. What shall I do, sir? I can't go on facin' Inspector Hartley. Him asking me all these questions. He's wearin' me down an' he knows it!"

Fawcett knew he had to act. She had to be got away.

"Look, Lizzie," he said. "Keep calm. Just keep calm and stay away from The Grange. I'm coming to bring you back to The Manor to stay with me. Now listen carefully and you'll be all right. Pack your bag and don't tell anyone where you're going. OK? I'll be down right away."

She'd nearly finished packing when a knock on the door startled her. She peered through the window. Inspector Hartley had returned. "My God!" she exclaimed and her heart began racing again. She kept quiet and didn't answer the door till he knocked again. She opened the door slightly, but it was enough for him to see in. "Going somewhere, Lizzie?" he asked casually, glancing round the room.

"Thought…thought I might get away for a few days," she mumbled. Her eyes were still red from weeping and it didn't escape his notice. He asked where, and she wiped her mouth with the back of her hand like a child. His eyes never left her face.

"If tha must know, I'm going to Mr Fawcett's," she blurted out. "He says I need a rest. This lot's gettin' me down, an' he says he'll take me in." She took out her hankie and started weeping again.

Hartley's eyes softened. "I don't like it no more than you, Lizzie," he said quietly. "But it's got to be sorted out for everybody's sake. And the quicker we get to the bottom of it all, the better."

He asked her how she was getting to Fawcett's place.

"He's coming to fetch me," she replied.

The inspector looked alarmed. "Is he, indeed?" he said. "Then tell him I'll be dropping by at the Manor before long, just to see how you're settling in. Now make sure to tell him that I'll be dropping by." Then he turned and left her at the door.

That night, Hartley and his wife were dining at the Khans. Over coffee after dinner, they began discussing the case. Blake Hartley said he was worried about Lizzie going to Grasby Manor. He was also worried about Sammy Woodley.

The inspector was convinced Quereshi had been sent to do a hit job. But his sergeant was puzzled. Why hadn't Quereshi killed Woodley, instead of it being the other way round? After all Quereshi was a professional. He'd a gun. Woodley was only a gardener and was unarmed.

"You underestimate Sammy, Khan," said the inspector. "There's more to folk than meets the eye. Sammy was next best thing to being a trained killer. He got Quereshi first. Jumped him before he knew what was happening. He knew the lie of the land and Quereshi didn't. Dropped him with his cross-bow, then finished him off by garrotting him. Now Fawcett won't rest till Sammy Woodley's dead. He knows too much. Which makes it imperative we reach Woodley before he does. He's our only hope to nail Fawcett...apart from Lizzie. And Fawcett's got her with him now."

"What're you going to do about her then, Blake?" asked Semina Khan.

"I'm going to take up Fawcett's invitation and visit Grasby Manor. You rather fancy the place, don't you, Khan? You can chat up the Hussein lady while I see how Lizzie Goodwin's settling in," he said with a wink at Semina.

Semina laughed, then asked if they were any nearer to finding Abdul Quereshi.

"No," said the inspector. "We've alerted Interpol, but we've heard nothing. If he'd gone back to Karachi, they'd have let us know. They're after him like us."

The conversation drifted to the hand-axes and the new evidence forensic had uncovered.

"Did Mrs Goodwin say anything about them?" asked Khan.

"No. Not a peep," said the inspector.

Semina Khan cut in. "I've been thinking about them," she said slowly. "If I'm right, there's more than one person involved in the old lady's murder."

Blake Hartley put down his cup. "Oh? How d'you make that out? Nothing points to more than one killer. The more folk involved in crime, the more clues they leave."

"You said there was a thumbprint on the handle of the murder weapon," she said.

"Aye. But it was too smudged to be of any use," Hartley replied.

"Which side of the handle was it on?" she asked.

The inspector thought for a moment. "I'm pretty sure the thumbprint was on the left side if the handle was held with blade forward."

"Then it must have been a right-handed person who replaced the hand-pike on the wall Yet you said from the angle of the blow to Miss Bradshaw's head the killer must have been left-handed," she said quietly.

"By Jove, you're right, Semina!" the inspector exclaimed.

"There's one in the eye for you, Blake," said his wife. "Feminine logic, which you're always on about, beats male hunches any time."

Blake Hartley smiled good-humouredly. "You're right, Semina," he said. "Absolutely right. It's so logical when you think about it. And it puts a whole new slant on the case, if a left-handed killer did the murder and a right-handed accomplice replaced the weapon."

"Any ideas, sir?" asked his sergeant.

Hartley shrugged his shoulders. "I'm relying on feminine logic to come up trumps," he said, smiling at his own wife. "All we have now is a left-handed murderer and a right-handed accomplice. Nothing more. Nothing less. I could hazard a guess, but I'm saying nowt. If I do that, I'm into non-factual data, as brother Arthur would say. And he wouldn't accept that at all. We know that Woodley and Fawcett were around on the night of the murder. We know Lizzie Goodwin was there shortly after. It's the bit inbetween that's missing. Those are the facts and we must stick to them." Then the inspector finished his coffee and sat back. "If you want guesswork, I'd have said it was Fawcett. He's calculating, clever and meticulously tidy. Exactly the sort who'd go to any length to cover his tracks. But he was miles away when his aunt was murdered. What's more, Donaldson won't hear a word said against him. If Fawcett *is* the killer, nothing short of a video recording of him doing the dirty deed will impress the Super…and even then he'd say we fixed it!"

# CHAPTER SEVENTEEN

Fawcett played a round of golf each Tuesday at the Royal Ridings Golf Club, on the way back from work. His business centred on a large warehouse, an old aircraft hangar from the war on a disused airfield. From there he distributed his antiques - and much else.

The Bradford police began surveilling his warehouse after they busted the Old Ram drugs ring. Fawcett was well aware he was being watched. What's more, he knew that they knew that he knew and he relished the situation. He loved living dangerously. It gave life more spice. It was all he lived for and part of his scenario was playing off people against each other.

Everything pointed in his direction as the mastermind behind the flow of drugs coming into the Riding. But Chief Superintendent Peters was helpless. The Old Boys network had him stymied. Fawcett knew so many top people and covered his tracks so well the Super had to tread very carefully. Very carefully indeed. From Peters all the way down to Donaldson the police had to watch their backs where Fawcett was concerned. Had he been in politics he'd have headed the cabinet.

What was worse, right under Peters' nose a new drug network was being built up. Narcotics were flowing up Airedale into Keighworth and beyond as easily as the river flowed down it. The Manchester Anti-drugs Squad were griping like mad. The stuff was coming over the Pennines into their patch by the bucketful.

Then by sheer chance, bumbling Blake Hartley found out who was running the drugs to Manchester.

Jock Swinford, the landlord of the Railway Tavern, alerted him first. The pub stood next to his church on the main road from Keighworth over the Pennines into Lancashire. For some time, Jock had noticed four strangers using his pub each Wednesday evening.

They kept themselves very much to themselves saying little to him beyond ordering their drinks. And that was strange. Normally, dour Northerners are a garrulous lot once they get going . They talk to anybody, especially in pubs.

So it was their stand-offishness which aroused his suspicion. Three would arrive about half-past six as the pub opened, and before the regulars came. Then they'd leave half-an-hour later after being joined by the fourth. They never ordered more than one drink and left straight after the fourth stranger had come in and met them

Jock suspected something was up and kept his eye on them through the bar mirror as he dried the glasses. One night he got the surprise of his life as money changed hands. Not in single notes - but bundles! In exchange a package went the other way. A package containing little plastic bags full of white powder.

One of the three to arrive first opened the package. He dipped his finger into a plastic bag and tasted the white powder. Then he nodded to his companions and resealed the package. They finished their drinks and left after giving the fourth man the bundles of cash, taking the package with them.

When he told Inspector Hartley about it, he guessed at once what they were up to. He'd stumbled on the Keighworth-Manchester run.

There were two bars in the pub. A tap-room where the locals played darts and pool, and the quieter saloon where the four strangers met. Jock also served meals in there for casual trade, usually motorists driving over the Pennines.

It was in the saloon that Blake Hartley set up a video camera hidden behind the bar, and the following Wednesday he got there in good time waiting for the men to arrive. He turned casually as they entered. One of them approached the bar to order drinks. Blake wished him good evening, but the other only nodded and grunted before returning to their table with the drinks. Blake continued speaking to the landlord, but his eyes never left the mirror and the three men behind him.

A few minutes later, a younger well-dressed man came in and joined the others. He carried an evening paper wrapped round a bulky package and placed it casually next to him on an empty seat where one of the others had put his paper. They spoke briefly, then the trio supped up and left quickly just as they'd always done, taking the newcomer's paper and leaving behind the newspaper they'd brought. The newcomer followed them a few minutes later, glancing quickly at the landlord but saying not a word.

"What d'you make of that, Blake?" said Jock.

"A drop, for certain," said Blake quietly. "Did you see how they did it?"

"Watched 'em like a hawk but I saw nowt," said the other.

"Did you see where the young'un put his paper?" asked Blake.

"On that empty chair. Out of the way," said Jock.

"Not *out* of the way, but *in* the way," replied the inspector. "The first paper held the money. The second the drugs. A double drop."

"Well, I never!" exclaimed the bemused landlord. "And right under our noses!"

They chatted a little longer then Blake collected his video and left. Outside there was no sign of the runners. But Jock had their car numbers. He'd taken them when he'd first become suspicious.

Blake Hartley paused outside the pub. It was dark but light streamed into the thickening dusk from the open porch of the church above him. The organist was practising and Bach's great Toccata and Fugue in G thundered into the night.

He stood listening a moment, before murmuring to himself, "God's beacon in a very dark world." Then he made his way home through the churchyard.

Next day he and Khan watched the video. When the runner arrived at the pub from Keighworth, Sergeant Khan stopped it to take a closer look. "I've seen that guy before," he said. "He works at the antiques shop in Chatsworth Street. He hasn't been there long but he gave Semina his card when we were last there. His name's Wayne Burrows. Quite a smooth operator. She'd have bought the whole shop if I hadn't been with her. Said he came from their Leeds branch."

Hartley grunted. "From Leeds, eh? Ten to one he's in Fawcett's set-up. But how's Fawcett getting the drugs to him in the first place? We've picked up everyone we know."

Khan asked if Donaldson had seen the video. Hartley said no, it would be asking for trouble. The superintendent couldn't keep his mouth shut and Fawcett would know in next to no time what was happening. In any case, Blake Hartley wanted Fawcett before the drugs squad picked him up. Wanted him badly for personal reasons.

"So, it's some sort of race between us and them, sir?" said Khan, looking keenly at his boss.

"Aye. You might say that, Khan," he muttered. But he avoided his sergeant's eye. "I think Peters ought to see the video. We owe him that. He might recognise the other characters on it and he deserves a break. He's up against it, like us."

He switched the video off, and began packing up. He said he was visiting Eli Cudworth that night. He'd been moved to a nursing home at Ilkesworth. Hartley had a hunch the old man could give them a lead.

As it was a pastoral visit, Hartley went to the nursing home wearing his clerical collar, and when he arrived he was surprised to find Eli already had a visitor, a middle-aged woman who sat holding his hand. She mistook the inspector for the local vicar and got up to go.

"Good evening," said the inspector. "I hope I'm not interrupting." He smiled at the woman.

Eli explained. "This is my daughter, Dorothy, boss. She's come down from Kendal."

Hartley shook her hand. "I can come back later," he offered.

"No, no, vicar," she said, "You've come just at the right time. I was leaving anyhow as I want to get back in the light." Then she turned back to her father and kissed him. "I'll see you on Saturday, Dad," she said. "Now just you think over what we've been talking about. You can't go back to an empty house in your condition. We've plenty of room at ours now that Billy's gone. And Fred says you're to come. You know what Fred's like. He won't take no for an answer."

She turned to Inspector Hartley and drew him to one side. "Perhaps he'll listen to you, vicar," she whispered. "Try and talk some sense into him. Me and Fred want him to come and live with us. But he's being stubborn. He just can't go on living by himself."

Hartley had heard it all before. He was constantly trying to reason with stubborn old folk who lived alone and didn't want to move. He said he'd do his best and wished her goodnight.

"You've a good lass there, Eli," he said gently.

"She wants me to go an' live wi' them," muttered Eli. "But I've always been independent an' I don't want to be a burden on 'em."

"I know," said the inspector. "And look where it's landed you. Best thing you could do now is to go and live with her. Old age comes to us all, Eli. Anyway, she'll keep you out of mischief. That's for sure. That's what daughters are for."

The old man smiled wanly. Said he'd think about it. And they chatted some time about his daughter's family before Hartley produced some stills from the video. Eli didn't recognise Wayne Burrows, but he did the other three. Knew them well.

"They've been running drugs for years," he said. "Though they front their drugs by dealing in antiques."

"And they're not the only ones," thought Hartley.

The old man gave the inspector their names. He wanted them nicked, the whole lot after what they'd done to him. He asked if they'd caught Woodley yet. Hartley said no. Then Eli surprised the inspector by telling him one of Woodley's relatives was in the nursing home. Indeed, he was in the same room sitting opposite. He told Hartley to have a word with him. He had something of interest to tell the inspector so Hartley wandered across.

He was a little old man, smaller even than Eli, shrinking into a huge armchair. He brightened visibly when the inspector approached, for he didn't get many visitors. Hartley drew up a chair.

"Eli tells me you're related to Sammy Woodley," the inspector began.

The other looked embarrassed. "Does tha know him well?" he asked cautiously.

"Not really," said Hartley. "More an acquaintance."

"Sammy's no real kin," offered the other, still regarding Hartley keenly. "He were fostered on us as a baby. Me mam were paid well to bring him up but me father never took to him. He weren't more'n a week or two owd when he were brought to us. Me mam were feeding our youngest at the time that's why they brought him to us. She wet-nursed babies for money when she'd had one herself." He lowered his voice more. "Tha see, Sammy were a chance-child. His father were some big-wig ower at Keighworth, so they said. We never found out who, but me mam an' dad were paid well to take Sammy off their hands an' give him our name."

Skeletons were beginning to rattle loudly in family cupboards, and Hartley listened intently.

"Payments allus came from a lawyer. A chap called Grimstone. A right slimy 'un if ever there was. Me mam could never abide him, an' it were him what said Sammy had to take our name. Course me dad didn't like it, but he did like t'payments they gave 'im every month. I allus felt sorry for Sammy for me father were a right bugger. He knocked us all about summat awful when he were in drink but he hated Sammy most of all. Once broke his leg an' Sammy finished up in 'ospital. It were never right afterwards, but that were all hushed up."

Hartley bit his lip and nodded. He asked if the old man knew what Woodley was called before he took their family name.

The other gazed blankly at the floor a moment, knitting his brows. Then he looked up. "Aye," he said slowly. "I do. It comes back now. Kirton he were called. The day he came, a woman in a posh car brought him. She let slip he were called Sammy Kirton, but that were never to be mentioned again. Me mam asked if he were christened. She were a reg'lar church-goer. T'other woman said she didn't know, so Sammy were christened, and his name were changed to ours."

"Kirton?" the inspector murmured. The name rang a bell.

Then it registered. It was Lizzie Goodwin's maiden name. And the unthinkable began to present itself. He knew Peter Fawcett had put a servant in the family way and been packed off till the scandal died down. But Lizzie Goodwin!

He recalled how attractive she'd once been. The snapshot on her cottage wall showed she'd once been a stunner. And he'd been surprised how blindly loyal she'd always been to Fawcett. She was still besotted with him. Yes. It all began to fit in place, and he almost reeled from the room after he'd wished Woodley and Eli goodnight.

The next day, he wasted no time obtaining a copy of Sammy Woodley's birth certificate. It confirmed all the old man had said, except for one thing. There was no father's name. The birth-certificate had Lizzie's maiden name all right, Elizabeth Kirton. And the hospital where Sammy was born. But the father was registered as "Unknown."

# CHAPTER EIGHTEEN

Ibrahim Khan played off a five handicap and had won a blue at Oxford. He still played golf and was delighted when an old college friend, just appointed a consultant at Leeds Infirmary, invited him to play at his new club, the Royal Ridings Golf Club.

Khan was glad to get away on his day off, for Donaldson had been on his back all week. He'd hardly been off it since the Old Ram bog-up. Along with Hartley he'd been carpeted yet again. This time Fawcett had complained they were inefficient, dragging their feet over his aunt's murder. He wasn't at all happy about it and cracked his masonic whip. And when Fawcett cracked his whip, Donaldson jumped to it - right onto their backs.

"The Chief Constable's been on the phone," he griped as soon as they'd entered his office. "He's breathing down my neck. And do you know why? Because he's got Peter Fawcett and the top brass he mixes with breathing down his neck. That's why!"

Khan looked subdued, but Hartley played deadpan, and that didn't help matters. He said nothing. Just sucked his lips and looked mulish, which irritated the Super immensely. What cards the inspector held he always played close to his chest. From the start, his attitude had been that the less his boss knew what was going on, the better.

So he'd said nothing about Fawcett being Sammy Woodley's father, and in any case it would have been the very devil of a job to prove. Grimstone had covered his tracks well. The birth certificate had clinched who was Woodley's mother - but the father? He was still non-factual data!

He wasn't factualised till a couple of days after the grilling Donaldson gave them. Not till Hartley ran across an old servant at The Grange. He came across her while he was visiting one of his parishioners in a Keighworth nursing home. She'd worked for the Bradshaws at the same time as his mother, and she confirmed all that Jack Woodley had said.

When she was in service at The Grange, she'd shared a room in the servants' quarters with Lizzie Kirton, as she was then. It was in her that Lizzie had confided when she'd become pregnant, the only one she dared talk to. She'd told her who the father was. It was Fawcett all right.

But it had to come out some time who was the father, and, as soon as the Bradshaws found out the situation, Lizzie was whisked away to a private clinic and the whole business was hushed up. It would have been more than her position was worth to speak about it then, so she told nobody. The secret remained between herself and Lizzie and the Fawcetts. As far as she knew, the baby was put in an orphanage and forgotten about, and when Lizzie came back, she was married off double-quick to the chauffeur Sam Goodwin. She never spoke about her child after that, but the old biddy said she grieved for him. She never had any more children and it was that which turned her mind, she said. She became a different woman altogether when she came back from the clinic.

The young Peter Fawcett also disappeared from the scene. He never came back during the holidays as he used to. Never returned for some years, in fact. But he wrote secretly to Lizzie and paid the old woman to be go-between. He always used to send Lizzie something on her birthday, she said, and it was odd he never forgot her. She reckoned it was he who forced his aunt, against her will, to keep Lizzie in service all those years.

Inspector Hartley said nothing of this to anyone, not even Khan. And the Bradshaw murder was the last thing Sergeant Khan wanted to think of when he went to play golf that day with his friend, Dr Alistair Stewart.

He'd mentioned Dr Stewart's appointment as a gastro-enterologist a few weeks before to Dr Dunwell when he and Hartley were lunching with the pathologist. Dr Stewart ranked high in Dr Dunwell's estimation, but as a result Khan had been regaled right through the main course to bowel malfunction. Dunwell omitted nothing. In the end, Khan just had to excuse himself and left the pathologist enthusing over the lower bowel with Hartley during dessert.

It was the first time Ibrahim Khan had played at the Royal Ridings. The club fees were way beyond him, but Superintendent Donaldson was a member there. He played weekly and always came back the next day with a new name to drop.

A long walnut and chrome bar greeted the members as they came in and the atmosphere was stiff with cigar smoke and brandy. So were the voices. The walls dripped with silver trophies and the carpet pile was deep and thick. It was a long chalk from the spartan club-room at Keighworth Golf Club, where Khan played.

The course, too, was out of this world. Immaculate bunkers. Manicured fairways. Landscaped settings. A Grecian idyll in golf. Leeds was out of sight over the skyline. Keighworth in another world. And Sergeant Khan savoured every moment.

But his idyll ended when he and Dr Stewart went into the bar afterwards. Lounging expansively against the bar barking his head off was Arthur Donaldson. By him stood Peter Fawcett with another character. It was difficult to say who was the more surprised, Khan or his boss

Donaldson had skived from the station, and was chatting with Fawcett and another of his favourite namings, Sir Henry Locke, the Deputy Lord Lieutenant. Donaldson was laughing loudly at some crack Fawcett had made. Khan's entrance wiped the smile off his face. He was lost for words, but Fawcett came to his rescue.

"Hello," he said smoothly, "if it isn't Sergeant Khan. You didn't tell me your sergeant was a member here, Arthur. We could have pulled him in for a foursome." He knew damned well Ibrahim Khan wasn't a member, but enjoyed pulling rank on Khan.

It took time for Donaldson to recover. Officially, he was still on duty but he'd skived off and he knew Khan knew it. He'd made a point many times at the station that he was on first names terms with Fawcett and his ilk. But now he heard his own Christian name used so familiarly in front of his sergeant, it threw him.

He hoped Khan would take the hint and push off. But he didn't. He stood his ground and made his boss sweat as Fawcett introduced him to Sir Henry. "This is one of Arthur's merry men," he quipped. "Sergeant Khan. As a matter of fact, he's been allocated to my poor aunt's case."

Sir Henry shook hands and Khan introduced his friend, explaining he was a consultant at the Infirmary. Donaldson pricked his ears. "Oh, I've a friend on the management board there," he said and went on to name him. "What are you a consultant in?" he asked next.

"Bowels!" said the doctor in his thickest Scots brogue.

There was an awkward silence, which Fawcett broke with, "Oh, really? How quaint." Then he changed the subject quickly and asked after Semina and if the chairs she'd bought matched their table. "Your wife's a lady of considerable taste, sergeant," he said, pouring on the charm as he prattled on for some time on the subject of the antique chairs and Semina's good taste. Then he said suddenly, "Any nearer solving my aunt's murder, sergeant?"

Khan picked up the mockery in his voice but ignored it.

"We plod on, sir," was all he said. "A clue here, a clue there. Yes, we plod on."

"Talking of plod, sergeant, how's Hartley coping? He rather irritated me the last time we met. No tact and even less diplomacy," said Fawcett.

It was Donaldson who replied. "I'm sorry about that, Peter, but you know what Hartley's like. Getting a bit long in the tooth and all that. He's an old-fashioned plodder but he gets results, even if he treads on a few toes in the process, eh sergeant?"

Donaldson glanced at Khan, but Khan didn't laugh like the others. He gave his boss a withering look and said quietly, "Oh, I wouldn't say that, sir. He's no plodder. Inspector Hartley can gallop when he wants. Many a smart Alec has thought he's pulled the wool over his eyes, only to find in the end he's caught him in his own web."

He switched his gaze to Fawcett and there was another awkward silence which even Fawcett couldn't break. It was left to Sir Henry this time. He asked Dr Stewart which part of Scotland he hailed from. He often went there fishing.

The doctor said his family came from Pitlochry, but they'd gone south when he was a boy. Donaldson's ears went up again. He was obsessed with his family name and claimed he was descended from Scottish aristocrats. Years before he'd paid some quack genealogist, whose advert he'd read in a county glossy, to trace his ancestry. He boasted he could go back five generations to the Hebrides. When he'd told Hartley and Khan and they were safely back inside their own office, the inspector had said he wished their boss would return there. Anywhere as long he left Keighworth.

On the strength of his family tree, Donaldson had joined the Keighworth Caledonian Society, sported a Macdonald kilt at their dinners and taken up Highland dancing with his wife Daphne. He jumped at the opportunity of declaring his Scottish connection.

"Does your family wear the Hunting Stewart or the Royal Stewart tartan?" he said.

Doctor Stewart looked at him disdainfully. "Never worn a kilt in my life," he said.

"And you a Scot!" Donaldson exclaimed, abashed.

"There's more to being Scottish than wearing a kilt," the doctor replied scornfully.

Donaldson was squashed. He lapsed into sulky silence. It was Sir Henry who revived the small-talk again as Fawcett looked at his watch.

"Time I was away," he said. "I've another call to make before I sign off tonight." He turned to Arthur Donaldson. "Oh, Arthur, I wonder if I could impose on you again. Would you mind awfully if I asked you to drop off something at Chatsworth Antiques for me? I seem to be asking you to do it rather a lot recently, but it's a busy time of year."

The superintendent said he wouldn't mind at all. No problem. It was on his way home. He'd be only too pleased.

Sir Henry left with Fawcett and the doctor had a phone call to make, so Khan was left alone briefly with his boss. Both felt awkward.

"I didn't expect to be bumping into you here, Khan," Donaldson began, "but in some ways I'm glad. It's given you the opportunity of seeing the kind of people Mr Fawcett mixes with and why I have to tread so carefully in the Bradshaw case. I don't think Hartley quite realises what thin ice he's treading on when he goes blundering in the way he does. He's been going at things in such a bullish way with Mr Fawcett. When you've the chance, tell him quietly what's what, will you? He'll take it better coming from you."

The sergeant barely masked his contempt. "With respect, sir, Inspector Hartley may be bullish, as you put it, but that's the way he gets results. He curries favour with no one. That's what makes him a good copper, if you see what I mean, sir."

Donaldson saw what he meant all right and was furious, but Dr Stewart came back just then. He could say nothing. Khan and his friend said they were going and Donaldson shook hands affably enough. But he was still fuming when he left the club-house to collect the package Fawcett wanted him to deliver.

# CHAPTER NINETEEN

It was too late when Fawcett realised he was being double-crossed by Jay Hussein. He left many of his arrangements with her, including getting Quereshi smuggled out of the country. She'd done it before. The traffic tended to come the other way, though, in another racket Fawcett was running. This time unknown to Fawcett she also booked herself a one-way ticket out to Pakistan. She'd had enough of him, as Ibrahim Khan had discovered that night they'd come in together to the restaurant, for she'd been having an affair with Abdul Quereshi for some time. Now he was homing in to Grasby Manor to clinch everything. He was macho and good-looking. A man many women hankered after and Jay Hussein had everything all men want - including her father's bank balance.

The strange thing was that Fawcett never rumbled them, especially as he'd never taken to the younger Quereshi, and the longer he stayed at the Manor, the less he liked him.. He envied him his youth. His own had long gone, though he clung tenaciously to what was left. Life seemed to be slipping past, accelerating away now he'd turned sixty; so he couldn't get rid of the younger man fast enough. Bringing Lizzie to the Manor was a shrewd move. He trusted her completely. He knew she'd keep an eye on things while he wasn't there and let him know if anything was amiss.

The only worry was that she provided the excuse for another visit by Inspector Hartley. That was the last thing he wanted. He felt less and less sure of himself the more he met the inspector. He knew he no longer had the measure of him. The servant's boy was now an experienced policeman dogging his every move.

And Hartley turned up at the Manor quite unexpectedly the day after Fawcett had met Khan at the golf club. Inspector Hartley was very apologetic and said he wouldn't stay long. As he was in the area, he'd merely dropped by, as Fawcett had suggested (and Fawcett now bitterly regretted having invited him) to see how Mrs Goodwin was settling in. Hartley also let drop that Woodley had been sighted again. It was only a question of time before he was picked up. During their conversation he mentioned the stolen money. Fawcett became irritated.

"Do you really have to press charges on that score, inspector?" he asked. "Dammit, you know what Lizzie's like and how my aunt kept her short. As far as I'm concerned, I'm more than happy to let the matter drop. It brings us no nearer solving the murder, does it?"

"It would have helped if she'd come clean earlier," the inspector replied tartly. "There is such a thing as obstructing the police, sir," he added.

"I know. I know," said Fawcett impatiently. "But you're a man of discretion…and a man of the cloth. You don't really have to follow this up, do you? If it'll help, I'll have a word with your superintendent."

"I'm sure Superintendent Donaldson would be only too pleased to help, sir. He's always delighted to help his friends. But I shouldn't trouble him. He's enough on his plate. You're quite right. There are more important leads to follow."

"Such as?" said Fawcett in spite of himself. He could have bitten his tongue out when he saw it register on the inspector's face.

"Well, sir," said Hartley slowly, "I don't really like to bring it up, but in the course of enquiries, we've learned someone was seen climbing over your garden wall some days ago, sir. Do you know anything about it? We were worried it might have been Woodley. We thought he might have made for the Manor, seeing as he knew you. And he's a very dangerous man.”

“It’s the first I’ve heard about it,” said Fawcett blandly. “Who reported it?”

“Mr Fothergill, your neighbour, sir. He was silaging at the time, just over the way there. A man crossed his field, and you know what Mr Fothergill’s like when he sees folk trespassing on his land. He’s very particular. He said the man climbed over your wall before he could get to him. But he was close enough to see he was dark-skinned like Woodley. Any idea who it may have been, sir?”

Fawcett shrugged his shoulders. “A tramp in all probability. We often get them mooching round. They know I’m a soft touch. I’ll ask my man. He deals with them. He’s never mentioned it, so it can’t have been that important.”

“You’re probably right, sir. But I just thought I’d check it out,” said Hartley preparing to leave.

Fawcett almost bundled him down the corridor, so eager was he to get rid of him. “Quite right, inspector,” he said. “I admire your thoroughness.” He went before Hartley to open the door, but the inspector stalled and stood blocking the entrance as if he’d something else on his mind.

“Thank you, sir,” he said. “It’s kind of you to say that. And I’m glad Lizzie’s settling in. She was quite stressed out the last time I saw her at The Grange.”

“I didn’t like her being there by herself. Not with Woodley on the loose. I hope you catch him soon, then we’ll all sleep more easily in our beds,” Fawcett replied, trying to edge Hartley through the door.

But the inspector wouldn’t budge. He scratched his face thoughtfully. “Oh, yes,” he said. “I nearly forgot. There is one other thing, Mr Fawcett. That vase we both looked at.”

“The one on the mantelpiece?”

“Yes, sir. I had another look at it. Did you know it had a false base?”

Fawcett looked hard at Hartley. “Yes. I explained to your sergeant. It was a funerary urn, made that way to hold the ashes of the dead. Why do you ask?”

Hartley pursed his lips. "We found traces of heroin in it, sir," he said quietly.

"Good God!" exclaimed Fawcett. "Never! I don't believe it! How on earth did it get there?"

"I thought you might be able to suggest a reason, sir," said Hartley. "You're very up on urns."

"Inspector, I don't find that funny," snarled Fawcett. "You aren't suggesting I had anything to do with it, are you?"

"Not at all, sir. I merely wondered if you could throw some light on how heroin got in there."

"That's ridiculous," said Fawcett. "How could I explain how heroin was found in it? Are you implying my aunt was some kind of drug-addict? The idea's preposterous!"

"It is, indeed, sir," agreed Hartley. "More likely The Grange was being used to peddle the stuff unknown to her, after she went odd. But Miss Bradshaw wasn't as odd as some people thought. She may have rumbled something was wrong. We know Woodley smoked cannabis. He may have been on harder stuff."

"He's always been my prime suspect for her murder," said Fawcett, desperately hoping the inspector would push off. "Why should anyone want to kill her? Unless she'd somehow found out he was pushing drugs."

"Why, indeed?" echoed Hartley.

Fawcett was rattled. He lit up a cigarette in the porch and Hartley noticed his hand was shaking. As he pulled away he waved cheerily from his car. Fawcett didn't respond. He only glared back as he watched him leave.

Once he was safely out of the way, Quereshi and Jay Hussein appeared. They both looked scared and Quereshi asked at once if the inspector suspected anything. Scarcely keeping his anger under wraps, Fawcett said icily, "You'll be relieved to learn it wasn't you he was after. It was Woodley. But I'm certain the fellow is onto something. He's known all along what we used my aunt's vases for, but he's waited till now to tell me. I wonder why?" He spoke more to himself than the other two. The tables were turned. Hartley was now playing with him, leading him on, waiting for the right moment to pounce.

"Are you sure he knows nothing about me?" Quereshi asked.

"For God's sake, how can he, man, if what you've said is right?" burst out Fawcett angrily. "And if he does, he'll keep it to himself. He's like that. Tight as an oyster. But you aren't as clever as you thought, old fellow. You were seen arriving by that fool Fothergill. If Hartley has cards like that up his sleeve, which one will he play next? We've got to get you away double-quick. When's the next run, Jay?" he added turning to his woman.

"Thursday," she replied.

"Then make certain he's on it," he said grimly. Then he turned to Quereshi. "Jay will take you to our rendez-vous in Hull overnight Wednesday. Then you'll be on board by first light Thursday. From there on you're on your own, Quereshi. All the way back home," he added with an icy smile.

Quereshi thanked him effusively, but Fawcett ignored him and poured himself a drink. Quereshi was the least of his worries. He just had to get Woodley before the police did.

He'd a shrewd idea where he was hiding and would go after him the next day. With much on his mind he left the other two and wandered into his study. There he phoned Superintendent Donaldson.

# CHAPTER TWENTY

"The Super wants to see you, sir, - at once," said the duty clerk as Hartley reported for duty the next day.

"Oh? Any idea what for?" asked the inspector.

"No, sir. But he's in a foul mood. Got it in for you good and proper. Said you were to go up the instant you got in," said the clerk.

On principle, Hartley didn't go up immediately. He went to his own office to see if Sergeant Khan could enlighten him. Khan said Donaldson had been buzzing every two minutes to see if the inspector had arrived. He was blowing his top over something but didn't say what. He was saving that for Hartley.

"Our mutual friend Fawcett without a doubt," said the inspector. "I rattled him no end when I visited him yesterday. He's a right creep, he is. Reminds me more and more of a couple of lines from Milton: 'All was false and hollow; though his tongue dropped manna, and could have made the worse appear the better.' "

"And who was Milton writing about?" asked Khan.

"Satan," answered the inspector.

"Better not quote that to the Super. It'll just about finish him," said the sergeant laughing.

But even as Hartley was about to quote again, the phone rang. Khan picked it up, then held it at arm's length. Donaldson's bark roared round the room.

"I thought I made it quite clear Inspector Hartley had to report to me the minute he arrived!" shouted Donaldson. "I've just seen him come in. Why isn't he here?"

"Tell him I've been taken short," whispered Hartley.

But the phone smacked down before Khan could reply. The inspector sighed and picked up the Bradshaw file. He was on his way out, ready for yet another roasting, when Sergeant Khan remarked casually, "Oh, by the way, sir. I bumped into Fawcett at the Royal Ridings Golf Club. Our Arthur was with him. D'you know, Fawcett has him eating from his hand. The Super even ferries antiques regularly for him to that shop in Chatsworth Street."

Blake stopped in the doorway, then came back. "Say that again, Khan," he said, "slowly."

Sgt Khan looked surprised. "All he said was that it would save him a double journey and a deal of trouble if Donaldson dropped off the odd parcel for him now and again. I saw Fawcett himself give him a package while I was there. He's using our Arthur, sir, as his carrier. If Fawcett had patted him on the head, he couldn't have looked more pleased."

"And he's been carting these parcels back every time they play golf? Tuesdays, isn't it?" said the inspector thoughtfully.

"Yes. Why do you ask?" asked Khan.

Hartley smiled enigmatically. "My dear Sergeant Khan, good Muslim though you are, you've saved my bacon!" Then he strode out leaving a very bemused Khan behind him wondering what he was talking about.

He went at the double to the Super's office, taking the stairs two at a time. The duty office had never seen him move so fast and thought the Super had already given him a good old bollocking over the phone. When he reached Donaldson's office, he knocked doubly hard at the door.

"Come in!" bellowed Donaldson. "And don't knock as though you're trying to break down my door!" Hartley walked in briskly.

"You know why I've sent for you, don't you, Hartley?" began Donaldson glaring at him.

The inspector raised his eyebrows. "No, sir," he said sweetly.

"Don't play the innocent with me! You know perfectly well. You went to see Mr Fawcett yesterday, didn't you?" said the Super.

"Yes, sir. I can't deny that," said Hartley..

"And you had quite a cosy chat with him, didn't you, Hartley?" continued Donaldson with heavy sarcasm.

The inspector looked hurt. He said they'd discussed routine matters. His guileless attitude riled Donaldson more. He got to his feet and began pacing behind his desk.

"He phoned me just after you left. He said you'd damned near accused him of murder - then drug-pushing into the bargain!" He waited for an answer, but the inspector stood mute. "Just what the hell are you playing at, Hartley? Talk about fools rushing in where angels fear to tread! You've queered your pitch this time good and proper. He says if you as much as show your face at the Manor again he'll sue for harassment. He's already spoken to the Chief Constable and I had him on my back yesterday, too. He wants you off the case."

"But I was only carrying out my duty, sir ," pleaded Hartley.

Donaldson sat down and put his head in his hands. When he spoke again it was with barely controlled rage. He told Hartley he knew only too well from the past how he went about his duty. Like a bull in a china shop. This time he'd over-stepped the mark.

"But all I said was that traces of heroin had been found in a vase belonging to his aunt. I simply asked him how it had got there. That's all, sir," said Hartley.

"That's all! That's all, he says!" the superintendent exploded. He was much smaller than Blake Hartley and when he got to his feet, kept going up on his toes. The angrier he became, the more he rattled the loose change in his pockets, too.

Then he gave Hartley a real roasting, telling him he'd made an utter cock-up of the case from the start. That he'd put all their heads on the block. That he was incompetent, useless, and ought to be pensioned off. And that in any case he might well find himself a pensioner sooner than he thought. He ended by telling the inspector never to contact Fawcett again.

"Let Khan handle him," he said. "He knows how to handle people like Fawcett."

"So I believe, sir," said Hartley to Donaldson's back. He'd gone to the window and was staring into space.

"What do you mean by that remark?" he growled, swinging round.

"I gather you played golf together, sir," said Hartley.

"We did not play golf together, Hartley," said the Super. "We met quite by chance in the club-house. All credit to Khan, he handled a difficult situation calmly...tactfully. Better than I'd have thought. Better than you. He has the makings of a good officer - if he doesn't pick up your ways!"

Donaldson worked himself up into a real old lather, and Blake let him rave on.

"This...this bluff Yorkshire act you always put on, it cuts no ice with me...or my friends. You lack finesse, Hartley, and it's finesse you have to use when you deal with folk like Fawcett. Understand?"

"Yes, sir. I understand. Only too well," the inspector said quietly. Then he remarked, "I also understand you've been asked to drop off packages for Fawcett recently, in Keighworth."

Donaldson was taken aback. "As a matter of act, yes," he said slowly. "But what's it got to do with you?"

"Always at the same shop, sir, the same day?" continued Hartley, ignoring his question.

"Yes," said the other, even more slowly. Hartley's sudden change of tone dragged out replies. "I do it as a favour to a friend." Then something clicked. "By God, Hartley, you're not trying to pull me into this drugs business, are you?"

"To be quite bullish, sir...yes," said the inspector, handing over the file he'd brought with him. "Would you mind looking through those photos there, sir, and tell me if you recognise anyone?"

"Look here…" Donaldson blustered, but vibes sent alarm bells ringing. Some instinct for self-survival told him to do as his inspector said. He opened the file slowly.

In it were the shots of the Manchester pushers and the antiques shop assistant. Donaldson pointed to him. "He's the one I give Fawcett's packages to. I don't know the others. Never seen 'em before," he said dully. His voice had lost its bark. He almost whimpered, "There's nothing wrong in that, is there?"

He knew the question was rhetorical even as he asked it. Hartley strung him out.

"You're quite sure you give the packages to him and no one else, sir?"

"For God's sake tell me, Hartley! Stop beating about the bush. Is there something I should know?" asked the superintendent bleakly.

"There's a great deal you should know, sir," began the inspector. "For starters, over the last three weeks at least, that assistant has been distributing drugs to a Manchester ring. He's the link the Bradford drug-squad were seeking. But Chief Superintendent Peters has been letting him run so that when he makes his move, he can go to the very top and catch the big fish. Whoever's supplying that assistant is the Big White Chief, the baron at the very top."

Arthur Donaldson stared blankly at the photograph then stewed for a good five minutes staring through the window at Town Hall Square, saying nothing. Blake watched him in silence. At length, the Super cleared his throat and turned, mopping his brow feverishly.

"I…er…I don't know what to say," he began, in a very small voice. "I'm completely lost for words. If you're right…"

"I *am* right," cut in Hartley firmly.

"Then I've made myself look a complete ass, haven't I? I'm up to my neck in it, aren't I? My God, why didn't I realise something was up? I'm an utter fool!" exclaimed Donaldson.

Inspector Hartley was tempted to say he'd known that for a long time, but for once he held his peace. "Do you mind if I sit, sir? I've a lot of weight on my feet," he said, "and you and I have got a lot of serious talking to do."

Donaldson gestured feebly to a chair the other side of the desk. Hartley was glad to sit down and when he'd settled himself, he explained how he'd videoed the gang at the Railway Tavern. He asked if his boss would like to see it.

"If you insist," he said weakly. He'd rather have drunk poison Then, looking as if he was going to throw up, he added, "I suppose I owe you an apology, Hartley."

"I suppose you do, sir," replied the inspector. "But let that pass. The fact is, you're over a barrel - and I want you off it. Because if I don't get you off it, Fawcett will go scot-free. And I want him...badly. More than anything else."

Donaldson looked up. The tone of his inspector's voice had not escaped him.

"You've got something personal against him, haven't you?" he asked.

Hartley wouldn't reply. He simply rubbed more salt in. "I wonder what Sir Henry Locke will say when he finds out?" he mused. Donaldson winced. "And the Chief Constable?" he added. His boss looked sicker. "As you rightly said yourself, sir, fools indeed rush in where angels fear to tread."

"Don't preach, Hartley. For God's sake, don't preach. It's bad enough as it is without you preaching. But what am I going to do? If you're wrong and I do nothing, I'm in a mess. If you're right, I'm in a bigger mess. And just when I was in line for promotion." He moaned softly himself and Blake Hartley thought for one terrible moment he was going to weep. But he didn't.

"You can always do another run, sir," said Hartley quietly.

"Are you serious?" said Donaldson. "Run drugs!"

"Aye, sir. It's the only way," Hartley continued. "Only by running the stuff next week, as if nothing had happened, can we nail Fawcett. He has no alibi if we open his package before delivering to the shop. You'll bring in the vital evidence, sir. And we can make it appear as if you're a decoy and we've known about it all the time. You'll go up in the eyes of the powers that be no end, sir. There's only Khan and myself know the truth."

Donaldson brightened visibly. "You're right," he said. "If you pull this off I'll be eternally grateful, Hartley."

"If you get your promotion, sir, so will we. *Our* gratitude will know no bounds," said Hartley. But before his boss could say anything, he went on, "Khan and I will be very discreet, sir. He's not picked up any of my bullish habits, I assure you."

Donaldson coughed uneasily. "I'm sorry I said that, Hartley. I was too hasty. Upset. I hope you'll forgive me," he said, as if the words choked him.

Blake Hartley gave him an old-fashioned look, and said they'd both best forget what had been said. He had to keep Donaldson sweet at all costs. He wanted Fawcett before the Bradford drug-squad picked him up. His boss was his only chance.

"So, sir, you'll play golf as usual with Fawcett next Tuesday, and bring whatever he gives you back here for Khan and myself to check out."

"Of course, of course," said Donaldson eagerly. "Anything else?" The relief in the superintendent's voice was palpable.

"Just to beg you to act normal, sir. Don't do anything to alert Fawcett. As a matter of fact, give him a buzz while I'm here. Tell him you've given me a right ticking off and that you're considering taking me off the case. Anything to sound normal. Grovel to him sir. I'm sure you know how."

"And you know how to rub my nose in it, don't you, Hartley?" growled Donaldson in spite of himself. But he did what Hartley said.

"Will that be all then, sir?" asked the inspector, picking up his file. His boss nodded and Blake went to the door. There he paused. "I'll get the duty sergeant to send you some tea up, sir," he said. "You look as though you need it." Then he went out, skipping down the steps.

The entire office downstairs looked up as he strolled through. But he said nothing, only telling the duty sergeant to take Donaldson his tea.

He entered his own office all smiles. "Well, sir, what did our Arthur say?" asked Khan, surprised.

"The master's roar became the schoolboy's whimper," he replied. "You got us all off a very sticky wicket when you mentioned he'd been bag-carrying for Fawcett."

His sergeant was flummoxed. The inspector showed him Burrows' photograph. "He's the one who collects from our Arthur each Tuesday. Got it?" said Hartley.

The penny dropped and Khan burst out laughing. "I don't believe it!" he said. "The Super a drug courier! But what are you going to do, sir?"

"Nothing. I'm leaving it all to him," said Hartley. "He's going to do a run again next Tuesday, but when he arrives here we're going to have a quick look-see before he takes Fawcett's package to Burrows."

"And if by chance he's clean?" asked Khan.

"Then Fawcett will have the last laugh on us all," replied Hartley.

# CHAPTER TWENTY ONE

Sammy Woodley had been seen near the ruins of Boltby Abbey, which stood on the fringes of Boltby Forest. The sergeant at Grasby police station unwittingly told Fawcett all he wanted to know about Sammy's movements and those of the police searching for him. So he had a clear run the night he went to get Sammy. He'd told the sergeant he was going to do a spot of night-fishing and didn't want to foul up any on-going police operation. But the sergeant gave him the go-ahead. They'd no night-time ops planned..

Woodley had gone underground in the graveyard of the abbey. He knew the area like the back of his hand, and the locals stayed well clear of the place, especially at night. They swore the place was haunted by a giant ghost hound, a geytrash.

Legend had it that centuries earlier a wolf-hound on leash had dragged the lord of the manor's son to his death, holding back as they leapt the river at a notorious place called the Strid, a mile or so upstream. There the river narrowed and swirled a raging whirlpool through a cleft in the rocks. The young hunter was the first of many trying to leap the narrow gap. Since his death, they said the hound's ghost raced howling along the banks looking for its dead master. Many of the locals living in the nearby village swore blind they'd heard it.

Sammy knew the area well, including the warren of vaults built by the monks to house their dead. The graveyard was stiff with sepulchres, and in one of them Woodley had his hideout before he moved to a cave deep in the woods.

When dusk fell on the day after Blake Hartley had called, Fawcett made his move. He went after Sammy armed with a hunting rifle with night-sights. He took with him Carter, the handyman, and the three wolf-hounds.

It was almost dark by the time they reached Bardby Tower to the west of the forest. The sky was clear and a full moon made their going easy once they left their estate car and set off on foot. The hounds were leashed and well trained, loping silently beside them as they hurried down the track to the river. In the distance they could hear the dull roar from the Strid drifting through the still evening air.

As light slipped away, the trees became mere silhouettes, the openings in them silvered by the moon. Nearer the river, the air became dank and the pungent smell of garlic hung heavy all about them. The shadows deepened till wood and scrub became one. In parts, the forest was almost impenetrable and the temperature dropped noticeably. Fawcett pulled up the collar of his shooting jacket.

Half an hour later they were near the cave where Woodley had his base-camp, where he'd killed Quereshi. Fawcett and his man separated. They'd no intention of being jumped like Quereshi, as they guessed Woodley would be armed. Fawcett took the two house-dogs and Carter the other. Then they fanned out.

When Carter was in place, Fawcett gestured at the cave and Carter released his hound. The brute checked a moment at the entrance before picking up Woodley's scent and entering. It emerged moments later carrying a dirty woollen balaclava helmet.

Fawcett breathed more freely and stood up. He held a pistol like Carter and they moved warily towards the cave. There was no sign of life, so they pushed aside the foliage which masked the entrance, flashing their torches in the blackness beyond. Woodley had left. There was only his gear.

"I bet he's gone to the abbey vault," said Fawcett, glancing around. "Let the hounds smell his helmet and get on to his scent. We'll know which way he took."

Carter slipped the animals from their leads and let them cast round. One of them picked up Woodley's scent and gave a deep-throated bay. The other two joined it, tails high, eager to be off.

"Quiet, Jack!" growled Carter, and the hound fell silent. Then "Find!" The trio took off like loosed arrows, their heads low, loping along the track Woodley had taken some time before.

They plunged through the undergrowth till they reached the path the walkers used. At night, it was safe enough for Sammy to go that way, and the hounds lost his scent among all the others. The overpowering smell of field garlic foxed them, too, but Fawcett knew where he was for the path led straight to the abbey.

They had to pass the Strid on the way there and as they approached it, the roar of the whirlpool grew louder. It drowned all other sounds: the hooting of the owls, the bark of a fox, even the distant roar of a lorry climbing Bardby Hill. From time to time they glimpsed the moon. It lit the way ahead, silvering the hounds as they passed through the clearings.

In minutes they were at the point where the river lunged between two great outcrops of rock. Over aeons, the cataract had forced the shoulders of the rock apart till they were a grown man's leap from one side to the other. .

Fawcett peered over. The moonlight had a strangely fascinating effect. The waters below were a silver cauldron beckoning to anyone looking in. "Don't get too close, sir," warned his man.

Fawcett heeded his advice and moved away.

At the edge of the forest, the woodland opened into meadows, beyond which stood the abbey ruins. Sheep dotted the fields on one side. On the other was the graveyard in shadow. And deep shadows hung like webs on broken cornices and staring windows of the ruined abbey. The roof had long gone, centuries before.

Nothing stirred, except the grazing sheep, breaking the uncanny silence with their coughs and occasional bleat. Before they crossed the fields, Fawcett assembled his rifle, fitting a silencer and lining up the night-sights on the abbey to check them. Then he ordered Carter to prime the hounds.

The handyman let them smell the balaclava again, then the hounds moved on, tugging madly at their leads. When they reached the edge of the graveyard, the leads were slipped and the two men stood back in the shadow to observe the hounds as they cast for Woodley's scent.

A hound picked it up and bayed. The others raced towards it but Fawcett ordered them to heel and leashed them again, allowing only one hound to follow the scent. He didn't want to lose all three if they got within range of Woodley's pistol.

They scrambled after the huge wolfhound which leapt the gravestones leaning at crazy angles all around. It went straight as a die to the opposite side of the cemetery. Fawcett and his man followed as fast as they could, moving from cover to cover. Every sense, every nerve straining to catch sound or sight of their quarry.

Finally, the hound came to halt at an abandoned sepulchre. A stone urn had toppled across the entrance, where rusty gates hung; one hanging from a single hinge. Behind them, steps strewn with dead leaves and rubble led to a vault below. A barbed wire fence surrounded the area and a notice warned it wasn't safe and told people to keep out.

The hound leapt the fence and slowly approached the entrance to the vault. There it paused, threw back its head and gave a long chilling howl. Then it turned and stood waiting for the others to catch up.

"Call him in, Carter!" hissed Fawcett. "Woodley's down there for sure." He unhitched his rifle, trembling with excitement. They hid behind a headstone about thirty paces away, as the hound returned. Fawcett smiled grimly to himself but said nothing as he fondled his rifle.

Below in the charnel-house their quarry crouched white-faced and terrified. All around him stood banks of stone coffins filled with mouldering bones. The air was heavy with death. Behind him ran a crumbling tunnel back to the abbey. Down it the monks had brought their dead to their final resting-place.

Sammy Woodley had been sleeping when the unearthly howl outside had dragged him from sleep. He sat bolt upright shivering with fear, clutching the pistol he'd taken from Quereshi. The hound bayed again. Its cry rolled eerily round and round the vault and his terror increased.

"It's…it's the geytrash!" he gasped. "It's come to get me!" Then he lay shivering, too frightened to move till he heard Carter's voice calling the hound off. He got to his feet and limped to the other end of the vault, ready to scurry down the tunnel. There he waited, his gun at the ready.

It seemed ages before Fawcett's voice came down. "Sammy? Are you there, Sammy?" he called quietly. "I've come to help you, Sammy. To get you safely away. Come out, Sammy. There's only me and Carter."

Woodley gripped his pistol fiercely. The anger which had replaced fear swept through him uncontrollably. He moved to the foot of the steps. "Tha'rt a bloody liar, Fawcett! Tha's no intention of gettin' me away. Tha sent Quereshi to kill me, but I'll get thee. I swear it. If it's the last thing I do! It's between me an' thee now!"

The moon lit up the gateway to the tomb and he saw what he thought was the silhouette of Fawcett's head peering round it. He raised his pistol and took careful aim. Then fired three shots in quick succession.

Above, Fawcett's hat was blasted from the end of the stick he'd put it on and poked round the gates.

"Well, that solves one problem," he muttered to himself. "Pity about the hat, though. I rather liked it."

He shouted again down to Sammy, "You're making a big mistake, Sammy. You can't hide out for ever. They'll get you in the end. So why not come out and let's talk things over? It's your only chance."

Woodley snarled an obscenity back, then moved quickly through the tunnel to the abbey. Having surfaced, he skirted the nave and climbed to the base of the yawning east window. There he'd have a good view of the graveyard and the sepulchre entrance where Fawcett was waiting for him. He could see someone quite clearly stooping behind a gravestone. It was Carter but he mistook him for Fawcett.

Woodley took aim and fired. Carter fell backwards, yelling with pain. Then Fawcett appeared with his rifle. Woodley ducked back just in time. Fawcett's shot ricocheted off the stonework where his head had been.

Then Woodley limped quickly round the blind side of the ruins and made for the track back to his base-camp. Fawcett saw him as he moved into the moonlight for an instant, but he had to stay behind tending his man's arm, which was bleeding freely.

Fawcett called in the hounds and applied a tourniquet round his man's wound. The hounds were raring to go but he daren't risk their being shot.

"Can you move your fingers?" he asked his man.

"Aye," he replied. "But it bloody hurts!"

"No bones broken. You're lucky, Carter. It could have been your head. Get back to the wagon and wait for me there."

Carter climbed to his feet and Fawcett set off in pursuit of Sammy, racing towards the Strid. After weeks of living rough Sammy's leg ached and he limped badly. Fawcett and the hounds soon began to catch him up.

Fawcett reckoned Woodley had two shots left, so he kept his distance and leashed the hounds, gaining on him step by step. He could pick him off at leisure when the time was ripe.

As they drew nearer, he could hear him gasping and caught another brief glance of him as he broke cover. They were almost at the Strid before he cornered him. Woodley had come to a halt, crouching behind a tree, sobbing and gulping in the damp air. Overhead an owl screeched and its cry was picked up by another. Before them the whirlpool roared and swirled.

Woodley felt sick. He sat hunched and gasping, his eyes glued on the track behind where he knew Fawcett was. pursuing him. He waited for him to come within range and as he topped the rise, fired his remaining shots blindly. The light was deceptive and they whistled harmlessly past. He pulled the trigger repeatedly. But there were only empty clicks which told both hunted and hunter that Sammy was out of ammunition.

Fawcett had a good view of Woodley. He calmly told his hounds to sit and raised his rifle to finish him off. But even as he took aim, another idea presented itself. He smiled cruelly and fired just above the gardener's head, splintering the branch he crouched under.

The Strid lay not far away. It would do his work for him and give him added pleasure into the bargain. Any bullet found in Woodley's body might be traced back to him. Hartley would rumble it at once and he feared him now.

"Get on your feet, Sammy," he shouted. "I'll give you a sporting chance. If you reach the Strid before the dogs, I'll call them off."

"Tha bastard!" screamed the other, standing up. "Tha'rt lakin' wi' me! Gerrit ower and done wi'. Shoot me now, like tha told Quereshi to do. Only I got him first."

"I don't know how you did it, but you did well there, Sammy. Congratulations!" shouted Fawcett. "You were very smart. But I'm not going to shoot you, Sammy. You'll have to run or else the hounds will finish you off. You know what they're like."

Woodley knew what they were like all right. He'd seen Carter feed them. He'd no choice and limped off as fast as he could. Fawcett watched him with the same cruel smile till he gauged the right moment to release the hounds. By then, Sammy had reached the slippery slope down to the Strid.

"Take him, Jack! Take him, Bess and Beauty!" snarled Fawcett, slipping their leads and urging them on. The three dogs lunged into the dark racing madly at the figure in front.

Sammy turned and saw them coming. "Oh, God help me!" he moaned. He struggled to the Strid, then halted at the brink. The leap was beyond him. He turned again and the hounds were upon him.

He caught the first one by the throat, in mid-air, ducking and trying to hold it off as it tore at his face. Then he lost his footing and fell, rolling over and over, wrestling with the hound as the other two savaged his legs.

They slid nearer and nearer the Strid so Fawcett called off his hounds, fearing they'd follow Woodley in. Two of them came back, but the other was locked to Sammy who'd entwined his fingers in the brute's collar as he tried to throttle it.

There was nothing to stop them once they'd started rolling down the slope. Their momentum took them on and on. Within seconds both had dropped out of sight over the lip of the whirlpool into the raging waters.

The smile left Fawcett's face. He put down his rifle and, stepping gingerly down the slope, peered over the edge. He saw nothing.

Only the moonlight jumped and flickered in the seething cauldron below. Of Woodley and his hound there was no sign. Their bodies were already being whirled round and round, battered to oblivion in the black watery depths below.

# CHAPTER TWENTY TWO

Superintendent Donaldson arranged for his long-time friend, the Deputy Chief Constable of the Ridings, to play golf with him the following Tuesday. He suddenly felt vulnerable having to meet Fawcett alone. He needed support and the Deputy Chief Constable also took Tuesdays off to play golf.

Deputy Chief Constable Burnett came from the same mould as Donaldson. They'd known each other for years and were at university together. Like Donaldson, Burnett had crawled his way to the top. He was a great one for pecking-orders and the higher the heights he reached, the more he pecked at those below.

Neither was popular with his colleagues, so they valued each other's company. They'd joined the force together and Donaldson had done Burnett one or two favours in the past. Since they'd never been in competition for the same perch, Burnett was always willing to help out. But Donaldson daren't for the life of him tell his pal why he wanted him specially as his partner at golf that day.

He made out he needed some one who could play well. They were up against stiff opposition. And he hinted at names which might well help them in their respective careers. Burnett jumped at the chance.

When they arrived, Fawcett was chatting with a high-flying business friend and suggested they make up a foursome. Donaldson agreed. It was the longest round of golf he'd ever played. Fawcett was unusually quiet and said nothing about his taking back a parcel till the very end. By that time Donaldson was almost praying. He was in a muck-sweat and made a hash of his game.

It didn't escape Fawcett's notice. Not much did. Nor the fact the Super, too, was uncommonly quiet. He asked him why as they strolled back to the clubhouse after their game. "You feeling all right, Arthur? You haven't said much all afternoon and you gave us a walk-over. Not like you at all. Got something on your mind?"

His question chilled Donaldson. But he pulled himself together and mentioned the first thing that came to mind - Blake Hartley. His inspector was never far from his thoughts. A constant nagging at the back of his mind. A thorn in his side.

"Oh, so that's it!" laughed Fawcett. "That's what's bugging you. I'm sorry I had to blow my top over the phone, Arthur. But really! The man's becoming intolerable. Forget it, Arthur. It's not your fault. We all have our crosses to bear. Anyhow, a little bird tells me he won't be with you much longer. The Chief Constable and I were chatting about him yesterday over lunch. He agrees. Hartley's gone too far this time."

That made Donaldson feel worse. He let Fawcett make all the small-talk. He sounded so confident, so self-assured, the Super began to entertain second thoughts. Could Hartley after all be wrong? Could he be landing himself in deeper by obeying his inspector? He wished to God he could have been a thousand miles away and never heard of Hartley - nor Fawcett.

"I gave him a good bollocking after you'd rung off, Peter," he said lamely and hoped Fawcett would move off the subject. But he didn't. He kept on and on all the time about Hartley. In the end Donaldson muttered something about making sure Hartley wouldn't trouble Fawcett any more.

"Too damned true he won't! I've never known a man so impertinent. Nobody's spoken to me like he did. The quicker he goes, the better. He's a disgrace to the force," said Fawcett with feeling.

It was hard keeping up the pretence, but when Fawcett began probing deeper, Donaldson felt positively ill. "Oh, by the way, Arthur, Hartley mentioned something about heroin being found at The Grange. Is it true? It's the first I knew of it."

Formerly Donaldson would have told him everything. Now he played canny. He merely grunted, "Oh, it's true all right. We think it was Woodley. He's into drugs. We know he smokes cannabis and he may be into something stronger."

"Any news of him yet, Arthur?"

"No," said Donaldson, who was finding it more and more difficult to keep going. He was dying to ask Fawcett if he wanted anything taking back to his shop in Keighworth. But to touch on that would alert him. Mercifully, the others caught them up and turned the conversation. But not until the last minute, when they were strolling across the car-park, did Fawcett ask his usual favour. By then the Super was feeling very, very sick.

The parcel Fawcett gave him was well packed in bubble-wrapping, and boxed. It was bulkier than any of the others and Donaldson couldn't resist asking what it contained. "For heaven's sake be careful with it, Arthur," Fawcett replied, handing it over. "It's Ming china. Worth a bomb."

Donaldson placed the parcel carefully in the boot of his car, said his goodbyes and drove off, excusing himself from their usual drink in the bar. He had urgent unfinished business to see to back at the station. He couldn't get away fast enough and put his foot down all the way to Leeds, but they were repairing the bridge at Headingley and he got caught in a queue. There he stewed, and the nagging thought kept running through his mind that the parcel was clean. He wanted to pull in and check it, but he daren't. There just had to be witnesses present when that package was opened.

As he waited his mind raced. "Suppose Hartley's got it all wrong? Suppose Fawcett really is innocent? Suppose he's realised what's happened and planted a dummy package? He's clever enough for that. He grilled me all the way round today. Suppose..." and a hundred other suppositions crossed his mind before the lights changed.

They turned green and he put his foot down. He hadn't gone far, when he became aware of a blue light flashing in his mirror. A cop on a motorbike drew alongside and flagged him down. Donaldson pulled over. The cop climbed off his bike and strolled across slowly - very slowly - pulling off his gloves and taking out his notebook. Donaldson fumed. He reached for his coat in the back of the car, feeling in the pockets for his ID It wasn't there. He'd changed coats at home.

"Now look, officer," he blustered. "I'm Superintendent Donaldson of the Keighworth CID. I'm in a desperate hurry and if I'm not back in Keighworth soon, there'll be all hell to pay."

"That may be as it may, sir," drawled the other in a thick West Riding accent. (He sounded much like Hartley.) "But I've my duty to do... and if you say who you are, you know the rules, sir, as well as myself. My own Super's very tight on rules. Very tight indeed, sir. You were speeding in a built-up area, sir, and you were not on duty, it seems." He glanced at the golf-clubs in the back of the estate-car.

Donaldson decided it was best to humour him. "No, you're quite right, officer. I'm not on duty. It's my day off. I've been playing golf...with the Deputy Chief Constable Burnett, as a matter of fact. You've heard of him, no doubt?"

"Aye. I've heard a lot about him, but I haven't had the pleasure of meeting him. Now if you don't mind, sir, I'd like a few details," was all the other said, giving Donaldson an odd look. Then he began questioning him and writing down his replies slowly.

In the end, Donaldson said in a squeaky voice, "Look officer. You have all the information you require. Now for God's sake let me get on. It's urgent!"

The traffic cop, put away his notebook and saluted before signalling him on. Donaldson kept his eyes glued to the mirror till the bike stopped tailing him. Then he put his foot down again.

He had a clear run through to Keighworth and the nearer he approached the town, the better he felt. By the time he pulled in to the station parking lot, he was more like his old self.

Hartley and Khan came out to meet him. "We've done it!" he exclaimed triumphantly, as he opened the back of his car. "The package is in here." The other two peered over his shoulder. "Fawcett fell for it hook, line and sinker. But for heaven's sake be careful when you open it. He says there's a piece of Ming in there, worth a fortune."

Hartley removed the package carefully from its box. Then they unwrapped the bubble-packing round the vase. When he took it out, they gasped. It *was* beautiful. Late Ming. A delicate blue and white baluster vase with a shallow domed cover.

"What a work of art!" the inspector said. "What a beautiful carriage for such deadly cargo."

He lifted off the lid and looked inside. It was empty.

"What's up?" asked Donaldson impatiently. He also peered in, squinting this way and that, like a bird as if he couldn't believe his eyes. Then he looked under the vase. "My God, Hartley! It's as clean as a whistle!" he said at length, and anger pumped into his face.

"Perhaps there's a false bottom, like those Indian vases," suggested Khan. "Shall I smash it and see?"

The Super's colour drained. "No! No!" he wailed quickly. "Don't touch it, Khan. He's tricked us. The blighter must have known. But how, Hartley?"

The inspector looked blank. He was as shattered as his boss. It was Khan who came up trumps when he had a second look at the bubble-packing. He held it up to the light. Inside each capsule were grains of heroin. Kilos of it packed all round the vase.

The sighs of relief of the inspector and the Super were audible. "Get on to the Bradford drug-squad at once, Khan," ordered Donaldson. "Tell Peters what we've found. Put this lot together again, Hartley, and I'll drop it at the shop as per usual. We'll pick up that gang when they turn up at the Railway Tavern tomorrow."

"What about Fawcett?" asked Sergeant Khan.

"Leave him to the drug-squad," said Donaldson. "I'd...I'd rather we weren't involved."

"He's mine!" interrupted Inspector Hartley.

"But what's he got to do with us now?" asked Donaldson.

"Everything, sir," Hartley replied grimly. "And I want him before anyone else gets their tabs on him. The superintendent shrugged his shoulders and backed down. "Well, we've nothing to lose," he said. "Fawcett won't have any clout now."

"He never had with me, sir," said Hartley sourly as he wrapped up the vase. Donaldson gave him a quick glance. But said nothing.

# CHAPTER TWENTY THREE

The drug-squad picked up Burrows and his contacts at the Railway Tavern. It sent many rats bolting for cover on both sides of the Pennines and the police had a field-day catching them. Inspector Hartley knew Burrows would sing and that the Bradford lot would arrest Fawcett before him if he didn't act. He made his move at once.

He set off early next day for Grasby Manor, but, for some reason he couldn't explain, the nearer he got to the place, the more depressed he felt. They'd recovered Sammy Woodley's body from the river, still locked to the wolfhound, and that had upset him immensely.

It didn't require much imagination to guess what had happened. Moreover, he'd have to tell Fawcett who Sammy was; and though he detested the man, he realised he wasn't looking forward to it at all.

More than that, now that the end of the case was in sight, he felt pangs of guilt. He'd relentlessly pursued Fawcett with a zeal fired, not by professionalism, but vengeance. He knew that early on in the case, but now he was finding it difficult to reconcile it with his conscience.

He decided on impulse not to drive through Skiproyd, but turned off instead at Stetton, crossing into Wharfedale. It was quieter that way. It would take him past the abbey and Boltby Forest, the way Fawcett had driven the night he'd hunted Woodley.

By day, the ruins were quite different from the gloomy pile they presented at night. In the sunshine, tourists wandered idly around, glued to guidebooks, and picnickers mottled the meadows along the river. Upstream, in the shallows, a solitary fly-fisherman cast for trout. The scene was idyllic.

The inspector drove to Bardby Tower, then took the by-road to Grasby. Near the roadside, not far from the tower, was the cottage where Sammy Woodley had been raised. Now, huge picture windows ran the length of a modernised living room. Extensions were tacked on at either end. The mean windows of the kitchen Woodley knew had been torn out and bulls-eyed. A polished teak door with brass lanterns either side of it had replaced the wormy thing which once hung there. The new owner, a quick-rich, futures dealer from London, had come up for the weekend with his live-in, and a Rover 2000 stood outside.

Fawcett was right. The world was a very different place from the one he and Hartley had been brought up in. It had changed, but they had not.

When the inspector arrived at the manor, he was expected. Lizzie Goodwin answered the door. There was no sign of Jay Hussein, but Carter was there, looking very pale and with his arm in a sling. Hartley raised his trilby and asked if Fawcett was in.

"Aye," she said coldly. "He's expecting thee."

She opened the door to let him pass and followed him in. No hound shadowed his heels this time. The only one he saw was inside, lying full length inside the door of the lounge. It made no move when he went in.

Lizzie seated herself next to it, subdued like the brute at her feet. She remained silent till the end of the visit, one hand on her lap, the other stroking the dog's head. Her eyes never left the detective nor Fawcett.

She nodded by way of introduction at Peter Fawcett, who stood with his back to the fire. He'd been drinking heavily all night and the change in his appearance was quite marked. He looked older, drawn. His face seemed to hang on one side and his eyes were bloodshot and heavy. He stooped a little and slurred his speech. The inspector wondered if he'd had some sort of stroke.

They stood eyeing each other a moment. Then Fawcett mumbled, "I knew you'd come, Hartley. That you'd be in at the kill."

The inspector asked him what he meant, though he knew full well.

"Let's put it this way, old fellow, you dug up a pit of worms for the drugs squad to peck at, and they've eaten the lot. I'm surprised they aren't here already. But you've beaten 'em. You haven't raced here to talk about drugs, have you, old fellow? You want to discuss us now. Chat about old times. Give me my come-uppance, eh? So how about a drink for old times' sake? Oh, come on, Hartley, old chap. Don't look so serious. I know you're not on duty now - and we're out of Lent. This is a social visit. Isn't it? I know you like a good whisky."

"If you insist," said Hartley, watching him closely.

"I do, old fellow. Sit down, my dear chap. Make yourself at home," continued Fawcett expansively. "It'll be the last chance we'll get to chat so cosily together." He went across to the Sheraton and poured a drink, taking it himself to the inspector.

"Anyone who likes a good whisky is a man after my own heart. Wherever did you pick up your good taste? Certainly not at The Grange."

Inspector Hartley ignored his question. He raised his tumbler and toasted him. "Slainte!"

"Slainte mhor!" Fawcett replied, raising his.

They sipped their whisky slowly, both of them enjoying the flavour. For the first time each took his eyes off the other as they looked into their tumblers and pondered their vintage malt.

It was Fawcett who spoke again, once he'd resumed his place by the fire.. The drink loosened his tongue. He told the inspector Jay Hussein had done a bunk with Quereshi, speaking at some length about how they'd double-crossed him. Then he suddenly changed tack and began talking about their youth together at The Grange. "Almost like old times, isn't it? Me, Lizzie, you. Only we're older. Much older. And the world is older, too. Quite changed. Not so much fun in it any more..."

"Have you heard about Sammy Woodley?" interrupted Hartley.

"What about him?" said Fawcett guardedly. "I suppose you've picked him up. He's given you a good run for your money."

"He's been picked up all right. From the river. Dead," said Blake.

Fawcett continued sipping his drink. "What happened?" he asked casually. "Suicide?"

"Hardly. They recovered another body with his," he nodded at the hound by Lizzie. He spoke in snatches. "One of your wolf-hounds. It attacked him. He was badly bitten about the head. They drowned together. It must have been a dreadful ending."

Fawcett said nothing. He glanced at Lizzie Goodwin, but she remained seated like a statue. No one said anything for a while and the clock on the wall ticked louder.

Fawcett sipped his drink and grew steadily more flushed. He hadn't shaved, nor was he wearing his fancy cravat. His neck looked scraggy, his beard grizzled. He'd suddenly aged.

"I'd like you to tell me how it happened," said the inspector at length. "Only you know - and your sidekick outside with his arm in a sling."

Fawcett's mood suddenly changed and he became angry and snarled, "Woodley was got rid of because he became a liability. He knew too much."

"And so he was bumped off by someone else as usual. You never did like getting your dainty hands dirty, did you, Fawcett? Your sort never do!" said Hartley fiercely.

His words bit deep. Fawcett glared angrily back before going to the Sheraton again to pour himself another drink. But when he reached the table, he opened the drawer and took out his pistol. He turned suddenly and levelled it at the inspector.

Hartley was taken aback. "Don't be a fool, Fawcett!" he said. "You'll never get away with it!"

The other smiled and kept the gun levelled at Hartley. "You enjoyed getting that in, didn't you? About never dirtying my hands. You've always had that cheap working-class chip on your shoulder like the rest of them who come up through the ranks. Well, I'm going to dirty my dainty hands now, Hartley. And it's going to give me great pleasure. It'll be worth every moment watching the servant's boy cringe. The shock. The pain. The mess."

Blake Hartley stayed calm, though his heart beat like mad. Despite himself, he felt the cold chill of fear and he sipped his drink to steady himself. All the time his eyes never left the other.

"That would be very sporting, wouldn't it? Like the time you used to blast the birds from your father's moor. Like when you hunted poor Woodley. The game's up, Fawcett. Why make it even dirtier at the end?" Then he added, "But you always were a poor loser, weren't you?"

Fawcett's hand tightened on his gun. "I wouldn't know," he countered. "I can't remember the last time I lost." He smiled and lowered the pistol as if something had just occurred to him. Something he wanted to say before he finished off Hartley. "Yes, I do remember now. I lost out to you years ago. Lost out from the beginning."

"Lost out to me? How?" said the inspector puzzled.

"I lost out to you because I envied you, Hartley. Envied you till it hurt when we were growing up as boys together at The Grange."

"What do you mean?" asked Hartley, more perplexed than ever.

Fawcett began to speak more quickly. "I envied you your family life. Your mother. Your friends Your knowledge of Keighworth. The town you were clearly part of. I envied you your mother and the neighbours you talked about down Garlic Lane. Most of all, I envied you your mother's love and your home. You were never sent away like me. You never had to pretend. Oh, I know you think I'm maudlin, but I'm not. I'm coming clean. I'm deadly serious, confessing."

He paused and gave a cynical laugh, placing his gun on the mantelpiece while he lit a cigarette. Hartley stayed calm, sipping his drink from time to time and letting Fawcett do all the talking.

At length Hartley said, "You smoked the same cigarettes the night Lizzie lied and said she'd seen Woodley. And you must have had a field-day watching us from that lay-by on the moor above The Grange. We hadn't a clue then who'd done the murder."

Fawcett blew out a cloud of blue smoke and smiled again. "Full marks, Hartley. You're absolutely right. That puffed-up idiot Donaldson said you were a plodder, but he was wrong. Completely wrong as always. But for him you'd have had me in the bag weeks ago. By the way, just out of interest, why when you hated his guts did you save his head?"

"Because I wanted yours," said Hartley.

"And you a priest." said Fawcett. "'Vengeance is mine,' saith the Lord. Not a mere priest's…and a second-class priest at that!"

Blake Hartley remained silent. Peter Fawcett had read his soul.

"So, old fellow, let me be the first - and only one - to congratulate you. You got me in the end, but, alas, look where it's got you. At the wrong end of my gun," said Fawcett laughing.

He noticed the inspector's tumbler was empty, so he told Lizzie to re-fill it. The hound dutifully followed her to the Sheraton, then back to her chair. Fawcett watched her serve him, then resumed.

"Yes, Blake Hartley, I envied you like hell as a boy; and I still do. I don't mind admitting it now," he paused and took a long pull at his whisky. "I watched you once, y'know. I'll never forget it. It was the first time it dawned on me how much I envied you. And my envy turned to hate. A natural progression, I suppose, if you believe in sin. Envy, hate, murder. The Cain in us coming out. You were in the back garden reading a book. You looked so contented, so happy. Then it clicked why I was envious. It was your contented happiness. I'd been kidding myself all the time that I despised you, because you were not one of us. You were working-class; born to serve. One of the lower orders as my late-lamented aunt would have said. Sounds odd these days, doesn't it?" He laughed tipsily. "Working class? The jolly old working-class. Where's it gone? And what's become of the upper-class when the likes of you are priests in the jolly old C of E? My God, the world's turned upside down!"

As he listened Hartley found his words ironic. Hartley had also envied, and his envy, too, had turned to hatred. He realised that now. He would have liked to have told Fawcett, but he didn't. He was too proud.

After another long drink of whisky, Fawcett continued. "In some ways we're very much alike, old fellow. Bookish. Artistic. Intelligent. We both like good food and drink. When I grew to man's estate, that was the first thing I recognised about you. You were intelligent and had good taste. I like to think some of it was picked up at The Grange. It put you apart from the others of your class.

You were, yet you were not, one of them. Somehow you were one of us, yet you were not. You were classless, Hartley.

Strange how our paths have crossed again. If I were a Muslim, like your sergeant, I would call it fate. But I don't believe in fate. Yet I knew as soon as that fool Donaldson put you in charge of the case the dice were weighted against me. You were after me from the start. Both of us knew that. But it wasn't I who murdered my aunt, I assure you, old fellow."

"I know," said the inspector, glancing at Lizzie Goodwin.

"Her?" said Fawcett. "How did you know?"

"She'd all the motives. You yourself said there had to be a motive for every crime. You had none. Perhaps Lizzie would tell me herself. How about it, Lizzie?"

" 'Ave I got to, sir?" she asked.

"Why not, Lizzie. No one will know now except us," Fawcett replied, picking up his gun.

Lizzie told all. How she'd killed Miss Bradshaw. How the old lady had been nagging and insulting her for weeks, though she knew Lizzie wasn't well and suffered bad headaches. The night she returned from bingo, her employer was particularly vicious. She stayed up late just to tell her she knew everything and was going to tell the police she'd rumbled Fawcett's drug racket. More than that, she was going to alter her will. Cut the lot of them out. Lizzie couldn't stand by and let her shop Mr Fawcett so she killed her. As she confessed, Lizzie began wringing her hands and wiping her mouth like a child. She was growing more and more distressed so Fawcett stepped in.

"There's no need to go on, Lizzie. You know the rest, Hartley," he said. "When I arrived it was all over. Lizzie had rung me in a panic. I cleaned up and told Lizzie what to tell the police when she'd given me time to get back here."

"You've trained her well," said the inspector.

"She's always been loyal," Fawcett replied.

"I know," said Hartley quietly. "I've known that for some time."

"What d'you mean?" said Fawcett, scowling. "You know what?"

"All about you and Lizzie in the past," said Blake.

"You've been listening to too much gossip, old fellow," said Fawcett, lighting another cigarette.

Hartley ignored him and turned to Lizzie. "You remember Sally Greenbank?" he said.

Lizzie began wiping her mouth again.

"Sally?" she said in a hushed voice. "Is she still alive?"

"Aye," said the inspector. "She's in a nursing home and I've been visiting her these past few weeks. She's told me everything. About the baby."

"My bairn! She told thee about my bairn!" exclaimed Lizzie.

"Aye. She told me who his father was. And I'd like his father to know what became of him. It's time he did," said the inspector, turning to Fawcett.

"My, my, old fellow, you have been busy, haven't you? Trawling the murky waters of the past," jeered Fawcett.

"The murky waters of the present demanded it, old fellow," Hartley riposted

Fawcett shrugged and smiled, but the inspector noticed how his hand had began to shake even more when he lit another cigarette. "As a matter of fact, Hartley, what did happen to Lizzie's baby, now that you've brought the matter up? It was all kept very much from me. Anathema to my mother and aunt."

"Do you really want to know?" asked Blake.

"Fire away, old fellow. But don't be too melodramatic. People are much more broad-minded these days, thank God."

Hartley spoke quickly, angered by Fawcett's sneering attitude. "The baby was farmed out to a labourer's family on the Boltby Estate. Your family lawyer, Grimstone, did all the necessary. He covered up well. He had the baby's name changed to that of the foster parents. Then Lizzie was married off, too, to make sure her name was changed. But later, years later, underneath all that family pride she set such store by, your aunt's conscience was pricked. She had the lad brought back to The Grange to oversee him. She never told anyone because by then he'd been badly knocked about by the brute who was his foster father. He was retarded. Crippled in body and mind."

Fawcett bit his lip. "I never knew. Nor did Lizzie. Who was the boy? We'd a procession of half-wits at The Grange. There was only Lizzie and Woodley at the end..." He stopped speaking in mid-sentence. A look of horror came into his face. "No! It couldn't be! It wasn't...it wasn't Sammy Woodley, was it?"

The inspector nodded. When Fawcett spoke again he was barely audible.

"My God, what have I done?" he said, then turned angrily on Hartley. "You knew what you were doing when you came here. But this goes beyond all revenge! Well, you've got your pound of flesh, inspector, and more. Now it's my turn."

Hartley saw Fawcett's finger tighten on the gun. He closed his eyes and waited for the shot. But when it came, it was Fawcett who lay sprawled on the floor. He'd put the pistol to his own head.

# CHAPTER TWENTY FOUR

Dr Augustus Dunwell took the Khans and Hartleys out to dinner at The Chesterton Arms Hotel to celebrate the successful closing of the Bradshaw case. The hotel was renowned for its traditional north country cuisine, and Dunwell had long promised his friends a meal there.

An old coaching inn, The Chesterton Arms stood on the Ilkesworth-Grasby road not far from Boltby Abbey. It was built of local stone and had an untrammelled attractive frontage covered by Virginia creeper at one corner. Waterfalls of flowers cascaded from old hay-feeders either side of the door, and an old mounting-block blossomed nasturtiums from a pair of barrels on the top. None of your fancy fairy-lights or plastic fol-de-rols mucked up its façade. Nor was there any plastic knickknackery inside.

Mine host was the eldest daughter of Lady Chesterton, an enterprising young woman who despite her aristocratic upbringing had gone into trade and made the hotel popular. She knew how to make money for her aristocratic connections carried clout with social-climbers on both sides of the Atlantic. Those who considered themselves somebody in the Ridings patronised it; and those who came from across the pond went there to tell their friends when they returned they'd met a real English duchess. Dunwell gave it his blessing because of its good cooking and traditional Yorkshire dishes.

This was odd, because Augustus Dunwell was a well-travelled, home counties man with very cosmopolitan tastes. Odder still was the fact that he and Arthur Donaldson had been educated at the same public school down south and were in the same Masonic Lodge. Donaldson was forever sporting his Amchester Old Boys tie and once took Dunwell to task for not wearing one. And shortly after the Super had arrived in Keighworth, he'd taken it upon himself to give the doctor some brotherly advice one night at a Lodge meeting. He'd told Dunwell he ought to move on or else he'd be stuck in a rut in Keighworth for the rest of his life. Something Donaldson himself dreaded. But the worthy doctor had retorted that he'd tried damned hard for years to find the right rut for himself and he'd found it now in Keighworth and he'd no intention of leaving it, thank you. Not even if it meant sharing it with the likes of Donaldson. From then on, they avoided each other like the plague.

Over dinner, Blake Hartley told them about that final encounter at the Manor. He was sure Fawcett meant to kill him. "What made him change his mind at the last moment, I'll never know," he said.

"How did Lizzie Goodwin react?" asked Semina.

Hartley took a deep breath. "She howled like a demented thing and threw herself over his body," said the inspector. "The hound went berserk and went for me. I had to shoot it with Facwett's gun."

They sipped their drinks in silence a while, then Dunwell said, "You've heard Lizzie has been sectioned to Hepston Hospital. She's quite unfit to plead."

"I know," said Hartley. "I'm taking one of her old neighbours to see her tomorrow. She's about the only person she'll talk to."

"D'you think Fawcett would have bumped her off in time like he did Woodley?" asked Ibrahim Khan.

"No," said Blake. "He could have done it earlier and got away with it. I honestly think he still loved her after a fashion. Not in the way he fancied younger women. Something much deeper. I think she was the only person he'd ever really loved. The only one who'd given him real love when he lived at The Grange. His mother and aunt

153

certainly didn't. They doted on him, but didn't give him the love he craved." The inspector leaned across and squeezed his wife's hand. "We all need love and when we don't get it, especially as children, things begin to go wrong in life."

The arrival of their meal changed their conversation. It was Pinwheel Pie. The pastry was superb, and Dunwell tucked in with gusto like all confirmed bachelors. When they'd got into their stride Hartley continued discussing the case.

"Aye, Fawcett was a desperately lonely man despite all his socialising and womanising. I thought I had him sized up, but I was wrong. In the end, he knew me better than I knew him. Perhaps that's why he didn't pull the trigger on me. I'd got him wrong to the end. All that I once wanted, he had. Yet all the time I had what he craved for but couldn't get. At the end, I suddenly realised how like each other we were. If somehow we could have connected earlier, we'd both have been different. But we couldn't. The class divide stood between us."

Mary sensed her husband was getting in deep and brought him back to the case. "You never explained how Fawcett managed to kid you he was at Grasby Manor after Lizzie Goodwin killed his aunt. I remember at the time saying he couldn't possibly have murdered his aunt because he wasn't there."

"You were right, love," said her husband. "But he wasn't at the Manor either. He was half way there when the murder took place. Lizzie Goodwin rang him in a panic and Jay Hussein took the call. Then she contacted Fawcett on his car-phone. He'd left The Grange some time before where he'd been arranging a drugs drop with Woodley. They left before Lizzie came back from bingo. But unknown to them, Miss Bradshaw had rumbled what was happening. She'd overheard her nephew and Woodley, because they didn't know she was still up, sitting by herself in the dark in the lounge. Afterwards Fawcett drove home, dropping off Woodley at Skiproyd to visit his lady friend. As soon as Fawcett heard what Lizzie had done, he turned round and went back to The Grange to clean up. It must have shocked him rigid, but he stayed calm. He primed Lizzie what to say and to wait before she phoned us. Then he cleared off as fast as he could back to Grasby."

"He must have had a fright," said Semina.

"Just the sort of situation he thrived on," said Hartley. "He drove like the devil back home. His car was plastered with mud the next day when we went to see him."

"Why did he say it had broken down?" asked Semina.

"Playing for time. He did some quick thinking to keep a step ahead of us. And, as it happened, I played straight into his hands saying I'd visit him the next day. It gave him all the time he needed to cook up an alibi."

They finished their meal and adjourned to the lounge. It was a large comfortable room and an aroma of freshly ground coffee met them as they entered. But barely had they settled down than familiar loud voices shattered their peace. Arthur Donaldson and Daphne and another couple came in.

"Oh, no!" groaned Dunwell, looking over his shoulder. "Heads down. Perhaps they won't see us."

They were too late. Donaldson nodded at them briefly, then began sucking up to Lady Chesterton's elegant daughter who ushered him and his friends to a private table in an alcove at the far end of the room.

"Our Arthur's with top-brass tonight," observed Hartley, who sat facing the alcove. "The Chief Constable and his wife."

The elegant young woman stayed with Donaldson's party for a while and made small-talk before disappearing. Then a couple of smiling waiters appeared and danced attendance at Donaldson's table for the rest of the evening. But before they started their meal, the Super came tripping across the lounge, smiling brightly at Hartley and the others.

"Just thought I'd pop across to say hello," he began. "Sir William sent me to congratulate you on the way you handled the Bradshaw business, Hartley. Very well done."

Hartley just nodded and Donaldson gave one of his nervous coughs. He drew closer to the inspector out of earshot of the others, who were looking studiously into their coffee cups.

"As a matter of fact, Hartley, you saved us all a great deal of embarrassment at the Lodge. It's people like Fawcett who get the

Masons a bad name, you know."

"Aye, sir," replied Hartley, looking his boss straight in the eye. "It's folks just like him."

Then he let one of his heavy silences fall. It unnerved Donaldson who began fiddling with his Old Amchesterian tie. "Well, I'd better be getting back," he said. "Lady Chesterton's joining us shortly. That was her daughter who greeted us just now. You'll have to excuse me."

He nodded at the ladies again and flitted off.

"A minnow running with salmon," murmured the inspector when Donaldson had left. "But who knows," he added, smiling and raising his hand to acknowledge the Chief Constable's wave, "our Arthur may well get his promotion yet. Then we'll all live happily ever after."

# Books In The Blake Hartley Series

1.     The Bradshaw Mystery

2.     The Museum Mystery

3.     The Marcham Mystery

4.     The Graveyard Mystery

5.     The Allotment Mystery

6.     Moorland Mystery

7.     The Scrap-Yard Mystery

8.     The Dance-Hall Mystery

9.     The Bandstand Mystery

10.     The Merchant Bank Mystery

17920962R00094

Printed in Poland
by Amazon Fulfillment
Poland Sp. z o.o., Wrocław